'Y...   you,
M...

He... with just enough honey at the edges to keep things interesting. She bent lower; she had to if she wanted to get a good look at his face.

'You're not as pretty as I'd been led to expect.'

'Give me time. Bruises fade.'

Rowan smiled at him then, careless and casual, and that smile…

That smile was a weapon.

'Mr West, let me drive you up to the house and have a medic take a look at you. My men are taking bets on how many ribs you've broken and whether you've lost your hearing. Odds are three to one that you're simply a very good lip-reader.'

'They just want to look at my lips.'

Jared let them curve and he knew what effect they had—of that she was certain.

'I get that a lot.'

'And I'm sure you use it to your best advantage.' She let her gaze linger, appreciating him, and after a slow count to three she stopped. 'The fact remains that I'd like someone to take a look at you.'

'Is that an order?'

'Do you take them?'

He smiled again. 'From you, I might.'

Kelly Hunter has always had a weakness for fairytales, fantasy worlds, and losing herself in a good book. She is married with two children, avoids cooking and cleaning and, despite the best efforts of her family, is no sports fan! Kelly is, however, a keen gardener and has a fondness for roses. Kelly was born in Australia and has travelled extensively. Although she enjoys living and working in different parts of the world, she still calls Australia home.

Books by Kelly Hunter

The Night Before Christmas
What the Bride Didn't Know
The One That Got Away
The Trouble with Valentine's
Cracking the Dating Code
Flirting with Intent
The Man She Loves to Hate
With This Fling...
Red-Hot Renegade
Untameable Rogue
Revealed: A Prince and a Pregnancy

**Visit the author profile page at
millsandboon.co.uk for more titles**

THE SPY
WHO TAMED ME

BY
KELLY HUNTER

Published in Great Britain 2015
by Mills & Boon, an imprint of Harlequin (UK) Limited,
Eton House, 18-24 Paradise Road, Richmond, Surrey, TW9 1SR

© 2015 Kelly Hunter

ISBN: 978-0-263-24862-3

Harlequin (UK) Limited's policy is to use papers that are natural,
renewable and recyclable products and made from wood grown in
sustainable forests. The logging and manufacturing processes conform
to the legal environmental regulations of the country of origin.

Printed and bound in Spain
by CPI, Barcelona

THE SPY
WHO TAMED ME

For my wonderful editor, Joanne Grant.
Thanks for your patience.

CHAPTER ONE

ROWAN FARRINGDON DREADED Sunday dinners with her parents. The tradition was a new one, instated exactly one month after her parents had retired and bought themselves a gleaming glory of a house that has all the showiness of a museum and no warmth whatsoever. Even the floral arrangements were formal.

She'd made a mistake two months ago, when she'd turned up with an armful of scented overblown cream-and butter-coloured roses and had had them relegated to the laundry sink—doubtless to be tossed out at her mother's earliest convenience.

She hadn't made that mistake again.

For some reason her mother loved this house, and insisted that Rowan—as her only child and heir—love the house as well.

Never going to happen.

Rowan's hurried 'I'm well set up already, Mum. Sell the house. Spend every last penny you have before you go, I really won't mind…' probably hadn't been the most politically sensible thought ever voiced, but Rowan had meant every word of it.

To say that Rowan and her mother neither knew nor understood each other was something of an understatement.

Four people graced the enormous round table at this particular evening's formal dinner. Rowan's mother, father, grandfather, and herself. Presumably the round table gave the impression that everyone sitting at it was of equal importance, but the actual conversation around the table told a different story.

Rowan shared a glance with her grandfather as her father launched into yet another monologue that revolved around dining with dignitaries and very important people she'd never heard of. Both her parents had been Army in her younger years, and had made the switch to foreign ambassador postings later on. They'd led the expat life for most of their lives, while Rowan had been largely left behind with her grandfather. His job hadn't exactly been geared towards the raising of children either—he'd been an Army general—but he'd never once left her behind and she loved him all the more for it.

Rowan's phone buzzed once from its pocket in her handbag, sitting on the side table where she'd put it when she arrived, and Rowan winced. She knew what was coming.

'I thought I asked you to turn that off?' her mother told her coolly, her almond-brown eyes hard with displeasure.

People often thought brown eyes were soft, liquid and lovely.

Not all of them.

'You know I can't.' Rowan rose. 'Excuse me. I have to take that.'

She took her phone and the information on it out into the hall and returned a minute or so later. She crossed to her bag and slung it over her shoulder.

'You're leaving?' Her mother's voice was flat with accusation rather than disappointment.

Rowan nodded.

'Trouble?' asked her grandfather.

'I'm covering for one of the other directors this week, while he's out of the country. One of his agents has just emerged from deep cover. We're bringing him in.'

'We barely see you any more,' her mother offered next—never mind that before they'd retired they'd barely seen her at all.

'You barely saw her during her childhood,' her grandfather told his daughter bluntly. 'At least when Rowan leaves at a moment's notice she gives us an explanation.'

There was enough truth in those words to make her mother's lips draw tight. Enough of a sting in them to make Rowan's memories clamour for attention.

'But it's my *birthday*,' Rowan had once said to her mother as her parents had headed out through the door, their travel bags rolling behind them like obedient pets. 'Grandfather made cake. He *made* it for us.'

'I'm sorry, dear,' her mother had said. 'Needs must.'

'But you've only been here one day,' she'd said to her father once, and had received a stern lecture on tolerance and duty for her efforts.

'Where are you going?'

She'd stopped asking that one. To this day she didn't think she'd ever received a truthful answer. The take-home message had always been that they were going somewhere important and that Rowan wasn't welcome.

'You need to toughen up,' her parents had told her over and over—and toughen up she had.

That her mother now wanted a different type of relationship with her only child concerned Rowan not at all.

'I'm sorry. I have to go.'

'Your grandfather's not getting any younger, Rowan. You could do more for him.'

Her mother's salvo had been designed to hurt, but Rowan just smiled politely and let it land on barren ground somewhere left of its target. Rowan saw her grandfather at least twice a week, and called him every other day and then some.

Not that her mother knew that.

Nor did Rowan feel the urge to enlighten her.

'You'd like this agent who's just arrived,' she told her grandfather, for she knew he'd be interested. 'He's been causing utter mayhem with very limited resources.'

'Is he ex-Army?'

'No, he's one of ours from the ground up. Very creative.'

Ten to one that the next time she called her grandfather he'd know who she was talking about. He might be long retired, but he still had impressive contacts.

'Yes, yes, Rowan. We *know* your job's important,' her mother said waspishly, and Rowan turned towards the immaculately coiffured woman who'd given birth to her.

For a woman who'd presumably had to fight the same gender battles that Rowan still fought, her mother appeared singularly unimpressed by Rowan's successes and the position she now held within the Australian Secret Intelligence Service.

'Enjoy your meal.' She managed a kiss for both her parents. 'I brought apple cobbler for dessert.'

'Did you make it yourself?'

One more barb from a mother who'd barely lifted a hand in the kitchen her entire life—such was the privileged expat existence she'd led.

'No. A friend of mine made it because I paid her to. It's her grandmother's recipe, passed down through the generations. I hope you like it.'

Dismissing her mother, she crossed next to her grandfather and placed a soft kiss on his cheek.

Her phone pinged again and Rowan straightened. 'Time to go.'

'I suppose that's your driver?' her mother said sarcastically. 'He's a little impatient.'

'No, he's just letting me know that he's here.'

'Maybe you'll see your way to staying for the entire meal next month. If I even bother to continue with these dinners.'

'Your call, Mother.' Rowan glanced towards her father, who'd sat uncharacteristically silent throughout the exchange. 'Are *you* displeased with me as well?'

Her father said nothing. Ever the diplomat.

'You know, Mother…both of you, come to think of it…just once you might want to try being proud of me and the position I hold instead of continually criticising my choices. Just once. Maybe then I'd give you the time of day you so clearly expect.'

And that, thought Rowan grimly, was the end of Sunday dinner with her parents.

Her grandfather stood, always the gentleman, and accompanied her into the hall and to the front door while her parents stayed behind. It wasn't his house—it was her mother's immaculate mausoleum—but it would never occur to her to afford her daughter the same kind of courtesy she'd spent a lifetime offering to others.

Her mother had been a well-respected foreign ambassador, for heaven's sake. Marissa Farringdon-Stuart *knew* how to honour others.

'Don't mind her,' Rowan's grandfather said gently.

'She's getting worse.'

'She's losing her grip on what's acceptable behaviour and what's not. Early onset dementia.'

'Nice try, old man, but I know what dementia is and what it's not.'

What her mother dispensed had nothing to do with dementia—it was carefully calculated vitriol.

'She's jealous, and some of that's my doing,' her grandfather said gruffly. 'I never had time for her. I learned from that mistake and made sure I had time for you. Plus, you've done extremely well in your chosen profession. Your mother's competitive. That irks her too.'

'And my father? What's *his* beef with me?'

'Who'd know?' There was no love lost between her grandfather and the man his daughter had chosen to marry. 'He's an idiot. Too much noble blood and not enough brain cells.'

'I'll call you tomorrow,' she murmured.

'You look beautiful this evening,' her grandfather told her gruffly.

'Flatterer.'

Rowan tried to look her best for Sunday dinner—her mother expected it—but there was no escaping the fact that her eyes were unfashionably slanted, her mouth was too wide and her ears stuck out rather a lot, no matter what she did with her hair. In the end she'd cut her hair pixie-short and to hell with her ears.

She could look 'interesting', at a pinch.

Give her half an hour and the right kind of make-up and she could even look arresting.

But she would never be beautiful.

'Take the apple cobbler home with you when you go.

Ask for it. She'll only toss it the first chance she gets, and I had Maddy make it especially for you. Extra cinnamon.'

'I'll save you some.'

'I'll hold you to it.' Rowan embraced her increasingly fragile grandfather. 'See you Wednesday?'

He nodded. 'And bring me carnage, politics or intrigue.'

Rowan stepped from the house and headed towards the waiting vehicle. 'You can be sure of that.'

CHAPTER TWO

HE'D MISSED BIRTHDAYS, two Christmases and two New Year's Eves, but he hadn't missed his sister's wedding. That had to count for something.

So he'd been slightly late and utterly filthy? His sister Lena had still slotted him into her wedding party without a moment's hesitation, before turning back to the celebrant and marrying his best friend, Trig—Adrian Sinclair.

That had been several hours ago now. The wedding dinner plates had long since been cleared away and the dancing was now in full flow beside the lazy snake of an Aussie river, with spotlit red gums soaring into the night sky. Jared had tried to be there in spirit as well as in body. He'd smiled until his jaw ached. He'd danced with the bride and he'd teased the groom. He'd stood until he couldn't stand any more, and then he'd sat beneath one of the big old gum trees, his back to the bark, and let the party happen around him.

It had to be mid-evening by now—with many of the guests gearing up to kick on well into the night. Jared, on the other hand, could feel the adrenalin seeping out of his body and leaving a bone-deep exhaustion in its wake. He needed to find a bed and lie in it for a few days, weeks, months… He needed to find a place to be, a place to stay.

Damon had offered the beach house, and, yeah, maybe that would work for a few days. But people had a habit of dropping by the beach house, and what Jared really wanted was to be alone.

He watched with faint interest as Trig headed his way with a woman in tow. She'd arrived about an hour ago and hadn't seemed the slightest bit perturbed that she'd missed the wedding ceremony or the food. Not a guest, he surmised. He didn't quite know *what* she was.

Immaculately dressed—he'd give her that. All class, with slender legs and a pair of high-heeled shoes that he figured had cost a small fortune. Both his sisters had gone through an expensive shoe phase. He recognised the look of them, even if he couldn't recognise the brand.

The shoes stopped in front of him and he looked up, his head resting against the tree trunk, steadying him, holding him.

Up close, he could see that the slender athletic form he'd been admiring had more miles on it than he'd thought. Up close, he could see that whoever had put this woman's face together had had one hell of a liking for the unusual. She had a wide, lush mouth that tilted up at the edges, and wide-set eyes that tilted up at the edges too. Her nose was small. Her brown hair was short and boyish. Her ears weren't big, but maybe—just maybe—they stuck out a little.

Together, her features made up a whole that was too odd to be classically beautiful and too arresting to be ignored.

'Jared, I want you to meet Rowan Farringdon,' Trig

said. 'The new Head of Counter-Surveillance, Section Five.'

Section Five. Jared tried to get his brain to work. Section Five was Eastern Europe, and when he'd left two years ago it had been headed up by Old Man Evans. Hard to say if she was going to be an ally Jared could use or not.

Probably not.

'Your reputation precedes you, Mr West.'

Her voice came at him gravel-rough, with just enough honey at the edges to keep things interesting. She bent lower; she had to if she wanted to get a good look at his face.

'You're not as pretty as I'd been led to expect.'

'Give me time. Bruises fade.'

She smiled at him then, careless and casual, and that smile…

That smile was a weapon.

'Your sister suggested that you might want a lift up to the house. I have a car here.'

He'd noticed it. Black. Sleek. Probably armour-plated.

'Why all the security for a wedding?' He'd noticed them—of course he had. Fully a quarter of the guests here tonight were Special Forces and plenty of them were packing. As was the woman standing in front of him.

'You know the answer to that one, cowboy.' She smiled again, more gently this time. 'We're here for you.'

'You're not my section head.'

'And for that I am truly grateful. You've made quite a mess. *Bravo.* But the fact remains that we're here to take you to Canberra and make sure nothing untoward happens to you along the way.'

'Give me the weekend and I'll go willingly.'

'Mr West...' It was a murmur shot through with indulgence. 'We're giving you tonight, and for that you should be grateful. You were due back two years ago.'

'Sorry I'm late.' Jared shot her a lazy grin, just to see if it would annoy her. 'You're young for a director.'

'I'm forty years old and cunning as an outhouse rat.'

She was ten years older than him.

'Like I said...'

Her laugh came low and unfettered and slid straight into the number one spot in the list of things he needed to make this woman do again.

'Don't underestimate me, Mr West. And I won't underestimate you.'

'Call me Jared,' he murmured, and then he caught Trig's sudden alertness and switched his attention to his oldest friend—who was now his brand-new brother-in-law.

'Jared...'

Trig looked faintly amused—or was it resigned? Maybe Trig had ESP, or maybe he'd simply known Jared so long that he could read every twitch, but somehow Trig had sensed his interest in this section head with the funny face and the whisky voice and the smile that was a weapon.

'No.'

'Yes.'

'Really bad idea.'

'I've had worse.' Jared turned his attention back to the director and smiled.

Rowan Farringdon wasn't slow on the uptake. 'Listen to your friend, Mr West. I'd chew you up and spit you out before breakfast.'

'I wouldn't complain.'

'Oh, but you would.'

Did the woman's lips *never* stop tilting towards a smile?

'If I get in that car with you am I going to end up at the farmhouse or in debrief?'

'At the farmhouse for tonight. I give you my word. You don't have to be in debrief until ten past nine to-morrow morning.'

'Any idea what they plan to do with me after that?'

Her expression grew guarded and in that moment he got a glimpse of the razor-sharp politicking that could make a woman section head at forty.

'I dare say that'll depend on the way you play your cards from here on in. You *can* play? Right?'

He was handsomer than she'd expected, thought Rowan—and she'd expected a lot. His body was big, and brutally honed for fighting, and the close-cropped black hair on his head only added to his formidable air. In contrast, his face could have graced billboards or movie screens, and his mouth had a ripeness to it that would leave lov-ers dreaming for just one more taste. Great jawline and cheekbones—and eyes that had seemed soft and liquid-bright whenever he looked at his sister, but were sharp and assessing now.

This was the man who'd singlehandedly destroyed a hundred-billion-dollar illegal arms empire. Single-handedly exposed a line of rot within the anti-terrorism unit he'd worked for that had stretched all the way to a sub-director's chair. The fallout had been spectacular, and there was fierce debate as to whether there was still more to come—whether he'd withheld information… saved the best until last.

She would have.

'Mr West, let me drive you up to the house and have a doctor take a look at you. My men are taking bets on how many ribs you've broken and whether or not you've lost your hearing. Odds are three to one at the moment that you're simply a very good lip-reader.'

'They just want to look at my lips.' Jared West let his lips curve into that lazy smile again. 'I get that a lot.'

'I'm sure you do. And I'm sure you use it to your best advantage.' She let her gaze linger on the lips in question, because they really *were* that good, but after a slow count to three she stopped and snapped her gaze back to his eyes. *Control*. She had it and she fully intended to keep it. 'The fact remains that we'd like someone to take a look at you.'

'Is that an order?'

'Do you take them?'

He smiled again. 'From you—I might.'

'You could use a Taser on him?' Trig suggested. 'That might work.'

'I could, but he looks rough enough already. If I killed him there'd be paperwork.'

'Director, would you mind if I had a word with the groom in private?' asked West.

He tried to make the words sound like a request—he did give her that. But he expected her to grant his request. That much was very clear.

Rowan wasn't going anywhere until she'd figured out his health status.

'Try over by the river,' she suggested. 'It's private there.'

'It's private here.'

'Mr West.' Gloves off, then, and to hell with protecting his ego. 'How about you stand up and prove to my people that you can still walk?'

His chin came out. His gaze was all fierce challenge—no weakness in it at all.

'I can walk.'

'I'd like to see that.'

But he didn't get up.

Pride was a bitch.

'See that he gets to the house. We've a doctor waiting for him.'

Rowan didn't wait for Trig's reply before heading towards her car. She knew what it was going to cost West to get moving again. She'd been monitoring his movements ever since Antonov's super-yacht had blown up. The trail of destruction he'd left in his wake and his relentless drive to get home in time for his sister's wedding had been truly spectacular. No sleep for the past fifty hours and he was beyond exhausted—his body was struggling to hold him upright.

The only thing *keeping* him upright was willpower.

This was a man who'd been streamed for command from the moment he'd taken his first special intelligence service entry exam. He'd excelled at every position they'd ever given him. And if you counted his time with Antonov as solo dark ops work, he'd excelled at that too. She'd been expecting a pretty face atop a fierce intellect—a will of iron and a predisposition towards making trouble.

She wasn't disappointed.

'Great walk,' Jared murmured as he watched her walk away, all confidence and sway. And he still liked her ears.

'*Can* you walk?' Trig wasn't going to be distracted.

'I think so. I just can't get up.'

Trig held out his arm and Jared grasped it—high near the elbow, a climber's grip. Next minute he was standing, and gasping, trying not to pass out or throw up or both. Two harsh breaths after that Lena materialised beside him, swathed in wedding dress white, with her hand wrapped around his other upper arm to keep him balanced.

'You're heading up to the house?' she wanted to know.

'In a bit.' There was the small matter of having to get there on his own two feet to consider first.

He *could* walk.

Couldn't he?

'Use the bed in the master bedroom.'

'You mean *your* bed?' Their wedding bed? *Unlikely.* 'Yeah—no. Pretty dress. Maybe you should step back a bit.'

She didn't, and he bit down hard on his nausea. Lena never had been inclined to do as she was told. She was a lot like him in that regard. Instead she stepped up into his space, put a hand to his cheek and studied him with worried eyes.

'You look awful. Like you've been through hell to get here. Tell me you're not going back?'

'I can't tell you that, Lena.'

She got that stubborn set about her jaw that boded well for no one.

'Got some cleaning up to do,' he offered gruffly. 'Nothing too strenuous.'

'Do you still have a job?'

'Could be I'm not flavour of the month.'

Trig snorted.

'What did the director say?' asked Lena next.

'That we're leaving tomorrow.'

'Did she tell you that there's a doctor waiting up at the house to check you over? She called for one two minutes after she laid eyes on you.'

'Women *will* fuss.'

'Don't you dare lay that line on me. Or on her, for that matter. If I'd walked into *your* wedding looking like you do you'd have dragged me to the hospital two minutes after I arrived.'

'I'm going,' he muttered. 'Stop looking at me as if I'll break.'

'I had a *year* of people looking at me like that.'

'*I* didn't look at you like that,' he protested faintly.

'Yeah, because *you weren't here*.'

'I'm here now. Lena.'

It sounded like a plea. It *was* a plea. For mercy. For absolution. And she really needed to step away from him soon—before he ruined her dress.

'I'm going. I'll find a bed. Do whatever the good doctor says.' He covered her hand with his own and leaned into her touch. A moment of weakness—a tell for those watching. And there were plenty watching this little exchange. 'I'm going. I was just enjoying the party, that's all.'

He took one breath and then another. Stepped forward.

And the world went black.

CHAPTER THREE

'STUBBORN, ISN'T HE?' Rowan said to the hovering bride, in an attempt to put her at ease, while a local doctor recently persuaded to make house calls ordered the groom and one of her agents to lay Jared West on his back on the bed.

The bedroom décor was a mix of rainbow meeting Venetian chic, and the unconscious Jared looked decidedly out of place in it—never mind his hastily cobbled together wedding attire. Once a wolf, always a wolf... no matter what clothes he wore.

'You have no idea,' Lena said glumly. 'I should have let you escort him to hospital the minute he got here.'

Jared's eyelids lifted mere millimetres—just long enough for him to glare at them momentarily before they lowered again.

'What's his name?' asked the doctor.

'Jared West,' said Lena. 'Pain in the arse *extraordinaire*.'

The doctor grabbed a small flashlight and bent towards the patient. 'Jared? You with me?'

Jared grunted what might have been a yes.

'I'm going to check your pupils for responsiveness to light. This won't hurt.'

'Not concussed. Concussion was three days ago. I'm over it,' Jared mumbled, but he proceeded to co-operate.

'Glad to hear it. Does that diagnosis come with a medical degree as well?'

'Comes with experience.'

'Is he always this argumentative?' Rowan asked Lena from the end of the bed.

'Yeah, that's him. He prefers to call it persuasion.'

'Got any bumps on the head?' the doctor asked his newest patient.

'Couple.'

Jared let the doctor examine them.

'What about your neck? Any stiffness there? Movement okay?'

Jared had his eyes closed when he answered. 'My neck's okay. Shoulder's wrecked.'

So much for the busted eardrums theory, thought Rowan with a sliver of relief. If Jared could answer the doc's quiet questions without watching the older man's lips, he wasn't deaf.

'You're not deaf,' she said, and was rewarded by the faintest curve of Jared's lips. 'There goes a week's wages for at least half of my agents.'

'Yeah, but the other half will be richer for it.'

'What's he like when he really smiles?' Rowan asked.

Maybe it wasn't an entirely appropriate question to voice, but it never hurt to be well informed and armed for the battles ahead.

'I haven't seen it for a while,' Lena said. 'But historically it tends to be pretty lethal. Nations fall. Angels weep. That sort of thing.'

'Amen,' Jared mumbled.

'See, if he wasn't all beat up I'd thump that arrogance out of him,' offered Lena. 'Because I love him.'

Her eyes filled with tears and she turned away before her brother could open *his* eyes and see them.

The doctor picked it up, though, and his next words were soothing. 'He's conscious, he's coherent—'

'No blood coming out of any orifices. I'm perfect... Got any painkillers?' the patient said next.

'For what?'

'Ribs.'

'Sit up and let's have a look at them.'

Jared moved to a sitting position on the edge of the bed with a little help from Trig. He also accepted help when it came to the removal of his borrowed suit jacket, but he unbuttoned the shirt beneath it himself.

He took his time, but Rowan figured that the delay had more to do with Jared's current lack of fine motor skills than with any real desire to delay the process. Finally the shirt came off, to reveal a sweat-stained bandage held in place with silver electrician's tape.

'I dislocated my shoulder at one point as well. But I got it back in.'

'Yourself?'

'A bathtub helped.'

'Jared, can you raise your arms above your head?'

'Last time I tried that I woke up two hours later, face-down on the deck.'

'When was that?'

'Three days ago.'

'Any additional problems since then?'

'A crucifying lack of sleep.'

'Jared, I'm going to check your lungs and heart. Then you're going to raise your arms for me while I do it all again, and then you're going to lie back down while I examine your ribs more thoroughly.'

Jared nodded.

Rowan tried to afford the man some privacy, but it was hard not to stare at the spectacular bruising that bloomed across his sculpted chest as the doctor unwound the bandage. He'd taken a beating, this man. And then some.

The doctor listened to his lungs and heart with a stethoscope and then poked and prodded around his stomach and lower still while everyone else stood and watched. And then, as the patient began to raise his arms and the doctor began to press on his ribs, he passed out again.

'May as well keep going,' said the doctor as he caught him and eased him back onto the bed with impressive nonchalance.

Jared came round moments later but stayed right where he was, encouraged to do so by the doctor's hand on his shoulder.

The examination continued and the doctor finally made comment. 'Without access to X-rays, I'm thinking he has four substantially cracked ribs.'

'Show-off,' muttered Lena, her voice ragged with worry. 'What else?'

'Soft tissue damage—as you can see. Probably some compression damage. Do we know what hit him?'

'We know there was a series of explosions on board a yacht, and we can reasonably assume that Jared was thrown around by them. He also drove a truck through a warehouse wall and rolled a four-wheel drive in the desert.'

That was all the detail a civilian doctor needed.

'All of which happened two to three days ago.' She looked at the physician. 'He's been travelling ever since. Does he need a hospital?'

'No,' said West. Conscious again. 'I've already been to one.'

Not by my reckoning. 'Where?'

'In…um…' His voice drifted off. 'Might have been Budapest. X-rays. Strobe lights. Everything. They gave me pills.'

'Sure it wasn't a disco?' she offered dryly.

'I like you,' he said.

'Can you remember the name of the pills?' the doctor asked.

Jared snorted. 'No. They were good, though. Kept the packet for future reference. Pocket.'

The doctor leaned down and rifled through the shirt on the floor, pulling out a small container. 'How many did they give you?'

'Five.'

'Two to three days ago, yes? It says here one a day. Where are the other two? And don't tell me you doubled up on them.'

So the patient said nothing.

'What are they?' asked Lena.

'Cocaine derivative. Explains his ability to keep going, perhaps. And why he's crashing so heavily now.'

'Yep,' Jared muttered. 'Sleep.'

And then abruptly he tried to sit up again, with limited success.

'Why are there strawberries? Am I in the bridal suite?'

'No,' Lena told him. 'You're in the spare room.'

Jared subsided somewhat, but kept eyeing the strawberries warily. 'And those? Growing in the giant stripy teacup?'

'What about them?'

'Why?' His voice conveyed vast layers of confusion and a complete inability to comprehend such a thing.

'Her house, her rules,' offered Rowan. 'Don't over-think it.'

His eyes opened to slits. 'Does *your* spare room have strawberries in it?'

'I don't have any room to spare.'

'You probably let people crash in your room instead.' His lips quirked. 'I like it.'

'Jared,' said Lena sternly. 'Director on deck, remember? Less flirting—more respect.'

'Why are you still here?' Jared asked. 'Shouldn't you be at your wedding reception? All I'm doing right now is going to bed.' His voice softened. 'It's okay. *I'm* okay. I made it here, didn't I? Don't make me regret the effort.'

'If you need a hospital, Jared, and you're lying about having been to one already, I swear on my new husband's soul that I will make you regret it.'

'She's vicious,' Jared told his best friend. 'I hope you factored that in?'

The groom smiled, wide and warm. 'Get some rest.'

'I would if you left.'

The bride and groom made their exit, with Lena glancing back over her shoulder and warning her errant brother to be good just before the door closed behind them.

Only then did Jared allow his face to reset into a grimace of pain. 'Hey, Doc? About those painkillers...'

'On a scale of one to ten—one being zero and ten being unbearable—how much pain are you in?'

'If I lie perfectly still I can get it down to about a seven.'

The doctor told him to stay in bed and rummaged through his black medical bag for two little blue pills. He got a glass of water to wash them down with.

'This is going to knock you out. You may shower in the morning when you wake. No sudden movements. Preferably no more boat explosions or motor vehicle incidents.'

He looked at the patient and expanded his list.

'No surfing, boxing, skydiving or martial arts training. No weights, rock-climbing or kayaking. Getting the picture?'

'Loud and clear.'

'Gentle swimming…floating, paddling. Pretend you're three again. Shouldn't be too hard, by the sound of it.'

Rowan *liked* this elderly smalltown doctor.

'Listen to what your body is telling you and you might just come out of this in better shape than you deserve.'

Rowan liked this doctor a *lot*. 'You're not looking for casual work on an as-needed basis, are you? Because your bedside manner could really work for us.'

'I'm two years away from retirement and I've seen everything I want to see and then some when it comes to medical emergencies. I don't need to see any more of those.'

Pity.

'Hey, Doc…' the patient mumbled. 'Do you think she's got a funny face? I think so. But I really like it.'

The doctor sighed. 'That'll be the painkillers kicking in.'

'Great voice too,' Jared told them next. 'Makes me think of sex. Does it make *you* think of sex?'

'Son, you need to get some rest. Stop fighting it.'

The doctor slid Rowan a glance, his smirk in no way hidden.

'You might want to leave before he proposes.'

'I might want to hear it for blackmail purposes.' Come to think of it, she might just want to hear it for her own selfish reasons.

But it was a moot point. The man on the bed was already asleep.

'Do we have the all-clear to fly him elsewhere in the morning?'

The doctor nodded. 'Get him X-rayed as soon as you can…keep him hydrated, keep an eye on him.'

'Thank you for your co-operation.'

'Not a problem—no matter what my wife says. Always a pleasure to help our special intelligence service.' The doctor smiled his charmingly distinguished smile. 'Who do I bill?'

Jared woke in a bed that didn't rock with the rhythm of the ocean. It wasn't his bed—he knew that much. His bed for the past two years had been a narrow bunk beside the engine room of Antonov's super-yacht. It had been a floating fortress, locked down so hard that no one had been able to get near it undetected, and it had been more than capable of sinking anything that tried.

His bed hadn't been soft, like this one, and his bunk-room sure as hell hadn't contained a chest of drawers beneath a wooden window. Was that a pot full of *strawberries* sitting on top of it? He thought he remembered being puzzled by them last night as well. Because…*why*?

He opened his eyes a little more, turned his head and discovered lime-coloured sheets and a floral magenta and green comforter. If this was a motel he was clearly in the lollipop suite—but he didn't think this *was* a motel.

He rolled over onto his back and winced at the pain that seared through his body. There'd been a doctor at some point last night. The doctor had told him that his estimate of two cracked ribs had been a little under. There'd been pills last night too, and then there'd been blessed oblivion.

He was at Lena's farmhouse. He remembered now.

And he could use a couple more of those painkillers.

He heard a door open and then footsteps that seemed to stop at the end of the bed. He opened his eyes a little more. *Pretty* was his first thought. *Funny* was his next.

It was the woman from last night. He remembered her mouth and her ears. He didn't remember her eyes being quite such a tawny vivid gold.

'You awake?'

He also remembered her voice. His body heartily approved of her voice. 'Mmm…'

She wasn't just any woman. She was a director of counter-intelligence and he was in deep trouble. She wore a white collared shirt, dark grey trousers and a thin silver-coloured necklace that looked as if it would break the minute someone tugged on it. She was older than him by a few years and then some, and he was attracted to her, aware of her, in a way that he hadn't been aware of a woman for a very long time.

'We met last night,' he offered, in a voice still thick with sleep.

'So we did.'

No rings on her wedding finger. No rings anywhere on those slender, expertly manicured fingers.

'Not sure I remember who you are, though. Memory's a little fuzzy.'

Could be he was winding her up—just a little. Could be he wanted to see if her eyes would flash with irritation at having to introduce herself again, section director being such a forgettable position and all.

But her eyes did not flash with irritation. Instead, crinkles formed at the edges of them as she smiled, slow and sure. 'Oh, you poor darling man. I knew you were confused last night, but I didn't know you were *that* far gone. I'm your sister's wedding caterer.'

'I see.'

He really *didn't* see.

'You don't remember begging me to give you a lift to the nearest motel?' She looked so guileless. Damn, she was good. 'Because I did. Take you to the nearest motel, I mean. But the night manager took one look at you and remembered that he didn't have any vacancies. I was a little sceptical, but he was very certain. He figured you were either going to puke all over the room or die in your sleep, or both, and apparently that's bad for business. Also, you had no ID. He didn't like that either.'

Jared smiled. He had no idea where she was going with this story, but he figured he might as well let her run with it. Or maybe he just liked hearing her voice.

'What happened after that?'

'I offered to take you to the hospital.' She leaned her forearms over the slatted wooden bed-end. 'To which you said an emphatic no. You then told me I had the sexiest mouth you'd ever seen.'

'I did?' He might have thought it. He didn't think he'd *said* it.

'I was swearing at you at the time. Trust me, I was surprised too.'

Jared let his gaze slide to her mouth, all shapely and tilted at the corners as if she was always ready to smile. "You shouldn't have been that surprised.'

'And *then*...' she said, and followed those words with a very long pause. 'Then you said that if I gave you a bed for the night you'd give me an orgasm I would never forget.'

'I— *What?*'

'I know. An offer too good to refuse, right? I mean... I have this mouth, you have that face... I think you've cracked a rib or four, but we could have worked around them. So I brought you here and offered you coffee, but you said if it wasn't Turkish you didn't want it. That's when I got my first inkling that we might not be soul mates.'

We might not be wha—?

He was almost awake, and thoroughly confused, and, okay, he might have offered her a good time at some point—it wasn't beyond the realms of possibility—and the coffee line sounded like him, but still...

'And then you told me that the ripples in my hair re-minded you of deep ocean waves—in the moonlight, no less—and I figured we might just be soul mates after all. I've been wrong before.'

'I did *not* say that. I would *never* say that. Your hair's too short for ripples. It's unrippleable.'

'I gave you a glass of milk and three prescription painkillers and you groaned your gratitude. It was a deep and growly groan. Very sexy. I still had faint hope of an exemplary orgasm. Ninety seconds later you were asleep.'

She was better at this game than he was. He was playing injured, for starters. But maybe, just maybe, she was the better player.

'You can stop now, Director. I know who you are.'

'Of course you do.' She shot him a very level gaze. 'You need to stop playing me for a fool, Mr West. You need to stop looking at my mouth. And then you need to pay attention to what I'm about to say.'

He eased into a sitting position, wincing as he slung his legs over the side of the bed. At least he still had his trousers on. He remembered bandages too, but maybe they'd been coming off rather than going on. Either way, they were nowhere to be seen. Neither were any of his other clothes. Possibly because they'd been filthy.

He eyed the suitcase in the corner with interest. 'I'm listening.'

'You need to know that there's no record that you were working for us during your time with Antonov. No one's going to claim you as their dark pony. You're on your own.'

That got his attention. He dragged his gaze from the suitcase back to the section director standing at the end of the bed. 'So you're throwing me under a bus?'

These things happened when you came back covered in filth rather than glory.

'I'm sorry,' she murmured, but she didn't deny it.

'I want to talk to my handler.'

'Then talk. Because right now the closest thing you have to a handler is me.'

'No offence, but I don't know you.'

'No offence taken, but I do hope there's *someone* in-house that you're willing to talk to. I'll be in your sister's kitchen, Mr West. As for you, it's time to get dressed. My people are almost ready to leave and you're coming with us.'

'I am?'

'Yes. Either willingly or not.' She smiled gently. 'We don't care.'

'You know, they never mentioned that in the brochure.'

This time she laughed. 'Maybe you should have read the fine print.'

If Jared had figured to slip quietly out of the farmhouse unnoticed, he'd been sadly mistaken. A big breakfast cook-up was in progress by the time he emerged from the bedroom, with his brother, Damon, wielding the tongs and his sister Poppy presiding over the flipping of fried eggs. The director was there too, sitting on a stool, sipping coffee and reading something on her computer, looking for all the world as if she had a place in his family—as if she was comfortable there.

He headed for the coffee machine. Looked at it and sighed. It was shiny, spanking new, and he had no idea what half the knobs on it did. 'Does this do double-shot espresso?'

'Only if you ask nicely,' said Damon's very pregnant wife.

Ruby was her name, and Jared eyed the bright green bow atop her head warily. She opened the lid of the coffee container and the aroma of freshly ground beans assaulted his nose and sent him straight back to a little coffee house in Istanbul.

Ruby obligingly waved the container beneath his nose. 'We can put this in a pot and make it Turkish-style, if that's your preference?'

'I'm beginning to understand why Damon married you.'

'You mean, it didn't instantly dawn on you?'

'Um…' Why was his world suddenly so full of beautiful smart-mouthed women? 'Turkish coffee would be great. I can make it.'

Ruby favoured him with a pretty smile. Jared risked a glance in Damon's direction before taking a careful step back. He liked women with pretty smiles. *He did.* He'd never before been scared of one, but there was a first time for everything.

'I…uh…I'm sorry I couldn't make it back for your wedding.'

'Play your cards right and you can be Damon's plus-one at the birth.'

Oh, dear God. She was probably joking. Hopefully she was joking. But he figured a change of subject wouldn't hurt. 'Anyone seen the newly happily married couple this morning?'

'They're still in bed.'

Jared winced. There was another image he really didn't want in his head.

'You don't approve?' asked Poppy.

'I do approve. I just don't want to think about it.'

'Very healthy,' his new sister-in-law murmured.

'If I whimper will you back off?'

'I didn't think terrorist-hunters whimpered.'

'This one does.'

He shuffled around to the kitchen side of the bench,

opened a couple of cupboards before finding a saucepan and dumping some water in it. Surprisingly, Ruby carefully shook a damn near perfect amount of ground coffee into it before putting the coffee tin back on the counter.

'How are you feeling?' asked Poppy.

'Good.' As if a rhinoceros had rolled on him. 'Peachy.'

And then Poppy was beside him, worming her way beneath his arm and hugging him carefully, and he closed his eyes and rested his cheek on her head as he gathered her in—because it *was* good to be home, and they had no idea how much he'd missed this, missed them, and for what?

He'd brought down the Antonov operation. So what? Another arms dealer would take Antonov's place. He'd exposed a few moles in high places, but he'd be a fool to think he'd exposed them all. He *knew* he hadn't exposed them all.

He opened his eyes to find Rowan Farringdon staring at him with puzzled eyes. He knew he was showing his weakness for family but he just didn't care any more. He closed his eyes and hugged Poppy tighter.

'Do I get one of those?'

The voice came from the doorway. Jared opened his eyes and looked straight at Lena. She looked well, if a little tousled, and her pretty floral sundress suited her. She looked happy.

'If you want,' he offered gruffly.

'I do want.'

Lena started towards him, a slight hitch in her step— no way was he going to call it a limp—and then he had his arms full of Lena and Poppy both.

'Got to do something to take that look off your face,' said Lena.

'What look?'

'The faraway one. You need to come back to us, Jare.'

'I *am* back.'

Lena stared at him intently for what felt like a very long time before silently shaking her head and stepping away and turning towards the director.

'When does he have to leave?'

'Five minutes ago.'

Poppy's big blue eyes were grave. 'How much trouble are you in?'

'Don't care.'

'Will you stay working for them?'

'Don't know.'

Poppy didn't care that they were having this conversation in front of Rowan Farringdon. Neither did Jared.

'Do you want to?'

He didn't answer. He didn't know.

Damon shoved a dripping bacon and egg sandwich in his hand. Jared extricated himself from Poppy and bit into it with relief. He didn't need a plate—he was an old hand at eating on the go.

'Ready when you are, Director.'

'I haven't finished my coffee yet.' *You haven't even had yours*, her look said. *I'm cutting you a break, here. Take it and shut the hell up.*

He shut the hell up.

He bit into his sandwich more slowly this time. Coffee appeared and he reached for it gratefully. One minute passed. Two minutes. They left him alone. They asked no more questions.

And then two suited men darkened the doorway and Rowan Farringdon shut her little silver computer and stood up.

'Agent West,' one of them said, and there was a measure of respect in the man's voice that Jared had never heard before. 'It's time to go.'

CHAPTER FOUR

ROWAN'S OFFICE WAS the same as the offices that housed the other five section directors. Large, as befitting her position, it also had a small apartment tucked in behind it, for when she worked around the clock and needed to freshen up with a shower and a change of clothes—or, indeed, catch a couple of hours' sleep after coming off a thirty-six-hour shift.

Jared wasn't strictly her responsibility any more. In all good conscience Rowan could have left him to Corbin to break or to fix. But she, like everyone else in the building, was uncommonly interested in whatever further information he might have to divulge.

Not that Jared West seemed inclined to divulge anything at all—at least not to Corbin.

Rowan gave yesterday's recording of Jared's debrief one last scathing glance before leaning back in her desk chair and tilting her head from one side to the other in an effort to ease the tension in her neck. It was only Tuesday morning, but she felt as if she'd been here for ever.

She reached for her headset and put it on. 'Sam, have Agent West see me as soon as he's out of debrief.'

Some people in this building wanted to hear a real debrief, not the fairytale version that Jared was out there spinning—and as of this morning Rowan had been given the task of earning his trust and breaking him open.

If she could.

Jared didn't get out of debrief until midday Wednesday, and if he never again saw the inside of that little white room with its one-way mirror it would still be too soon.

Rowan Farringdon's request caught up with him two minutes later. Five minutes after that he was standing in her outer office, staring at a lionfish in a wall-sized fish tank while her plump and pretty assistant buzzed him in.

He liked it that she didn't keep him waiting. He liked it that she stayed seated behind her desk, because it re-inforced their respective positions within the service. They weren't equals here. He didn't expect them to be.

He stood before her desk, feet slightly apart, hands behind his back, and waited while she looked him over in silence. The bruises on his face combined purple with a sickly shade of yellow. He wondered if she thought him any prettier.

She got more arresting every time he saw her. Today she wore dark grey tailored trousers and a fitted shirt that had two layers—the inside layer a soft-looking dove-grey cotton, the outside layer a fine white silk. She looked comfortable in her clothes, her skin and her surroundings. Power suited her.

And Jared…Jared had *always* been attracted to power.

She gave him approximately three seconds to settle before looking up from her paperwork and getting to the point. 'Mr West, your debrief is a joke. Everyone knows it; not everyone's happy about it. Who *do* you intend to confide in?'

No one.

'I want to talk to my handler,' he said instead. 'I told Corbin that. I've told you this before as well. How many times do I have to say it?'

'I'm sorry.' She looked momentarily torn. 'Serrin's dead. He's been dead for two months.'

Jared kept his shoulders square and his face stony. This blow wouldn't break him. He was just…tired. Tired of all the games. Tired of dealing on his own and making mistakes that cost other people too much.

'Was it me? Did I leave him exposed?'

'Yours wasn't the only dark operation on Serrin's books. He came unstuck elsewhere.'

One less stain for Jared's soul. Assuming she was telling the truth.

She tilted her head to one side, her eyes searching and her smile oddly compassionate. 'Jared, things would go a lot easier if you could bring yourself to trust me.'

'I really don't do trust.'

'I know. I've read your file. Very few people are even allowed into your life, never mind privy to your thoughts. Your mother died giving birth to your brother. You're fiercely protective of your sisters, not so much your father or your brother, who you blame—just a little—for your mother's death. The only other emotional attachment you've ever made in your thirty years of living is to Trig Sinclair. You accepted *him* into your family unit when you were five.'

She still wasn't wearing any rings on those expertly manicured fingers.

'Here's the problem,' she continued. 'A lot of people around here think that you haven't quite finished exposing Antonov's reach. A lot of people want to help you finish what you started. So here are my questions, given that you're disinclined to share details. What are you waiting for? What do you need?'

A break, he wanted to say. *Absolution*. But he doubted she could give him either. 'I need to go to Belarus,' he said instead. Would she do it? Belarus was within her jurisdiction—her part of the world to monitor. 'Just for a few days. Corbin won't send me and I don't know why.'

She laughed, and it was still one of the nicest sounds he'd ever heard. 'Jared, have you *seen* your latest psych report?'

He hadn't seen it. Chances were he wasn't *going* to see it. 'What does it say?'

'That you have attachment issues, delusions of autonomy and a well-developed death wish. Corbin's not going to send you to Belarus. He's going to have a hard time sending you to the bathroom alone. All those sharp edges.'

'I am *not* suicidal.'

'Tell me what you want done in Belarus and I'll put someone on it. Discreetly. You can run them from here.'

'I don't work that way.'

'No? Maybe you should.'

She stood and headed for the door, but he wasn't ready for this interview to be over, and he hadn't yet let go of the rough edges he'd acquired after two years playing thug for Antonov.

He shot out his hand to keep the door closed and got up in her face.

Up close, he saw her eyes had little flecks of chocolate-brown in amongst the amber. He could smell the fresh lemon scent of her hair, feel the puff of her breath against his lips, and he knew that he was too close, that his lips were far too close to hers. Another inch and he'd be tasting her—and he wanted to. God. He wanted to fall into this woman and take his own sweet time climbing back out, and it didn't matter that she was a section head or that his behaviour was way out of line. Maybe he'd forgotten what normal behaviour was. Meet a woman, like a woman, ask her on a date. Maybe he should start there.

'Have dinner with me.'

'*That's* your next play?'

Nice to know he could surprise her. 'Why not?' He could feel the warmth in her, sense the steel in her, and he wanted both. 'You can toy with me. Mentor me. Discipline me. I'm young. Impulsive. Smitten.'

'I'm not.'

'Could be why I like you.' He eased back, just a fraction, and watched for signs of arousal in her—the faint flush of her skin or the hitch of her breath—but he didn't find any. Just a soul-deep caution that matched his own.

'You need to back off, Agent West.'

'How about I take you to lunch? I promise to behave.'

'No.' She pushed her knuckles into his injured ribs—not hard, but a warning nonetheless. 'You're out of line.'

'Would you hurt me?' He leaned into her hand. 'I don't think you would.'

'I'd rather not have to. Doesn't mean I won't, Mr West—'

'Call me Jared. Call me by my name.' He hadn't answered to his real name for such a long time—two years or thereabouts. He'd been Jimmy. Jimmy Bead. 'Just—use my name. The way you did before. I want to hear people say it.'

'Is your last name not enough?'

'First name's better.'

'Why?'

'There's more *me* in it.'

'Jared—'

'Yeah. That's the one.'

He stepped back all the way this time, and gave her the room she deserved. Her hand fell away and he felt the loss of warmth as if someone had dipped him in the Atlantic. He had a feeling that his psych report hadn't covered half of what was wrong with him at the moment.

Or maybe it had.

'If I say that my next question is for your benefit as well as mine, will you believe me?' she asked quietly.

He ran a hand through his hair. He'd been doing that of late too, and it wasn't something he'd ever done before— either as Jared or as JB...Jimmy Bead. 'What's the question?'

'Do you know who you're hunting? Antonov's last insider... Do you know who it is?'

'I— No. I think it's a director, but I don't know who it is. If I could have nailed a bullseye to his forehead I'd have done it.'

'That much I *do* believe.'

'Get me to Belarus,' he begged.

'No. Not yet. You need to rest. Take some leave. No one's going to send you back out into the field in the condition you're in. Get some sleep and let your body heal and *then* we'll talk again. And, Jared...?'

'That's me,' he muttered, and there was a joke in there somewhere, though it was probably on him.

'Welcome back.'

CHAPTER FIVE

THE WEST FAMILY beach house sat on the edge of a long stretch of unpatrolled beach in northern New South Wales. Jared's brother had bought the sprawling house several years ago, with the intention of making it his home, but that hadn't happened yet and all four West siblings tended to treat it as their own personal place of sanctuary and of rest. Although preferably not all at once.

Lena and Trig's big old farmhouse was a twenty-minute drive away, although given how much time they'd spent at the beach house with Jared this week he could be forgiven for thinking them homeless.

They were supposed to be on their honeymoon, for heaven's sake. A honeymoon that Lena had said they'd cut short because there was no place like home.

Jared hoped, for the umpteenth time, that they hadn't cut it short because they'd wanted to keep an eye on *him*. They kept making excuses to drop by. Lena in particular wouldn't stop *hovering*—which was rich, given how much she hated it whenever someone did that to her.

She had already been by this morning. She'd skipped out to the shops, because apparently Jared needed more food in the fridge, but she'd left Trig behind with Jared.

Trig was currently out on the deck, examining his parachute, because apparently they were doing a jump just as soon as Jared's ribs had healed.

Without physical challenge in his life, Jared got cranky, Trig had informed him blithely. And they needed to fix that.

Apparently a lot of things about Jared needed fixing.

Jared glared afresh at the psych report in his hand. *His* psych report, fresh off the back of his debrief. A normal person probably wouldn't have asked his brother to swipe a psych report from the secure ASIS databanks, but to Jared's way of thinking that was what genius younger brothers were for.

It had been three days since Rowan Farringdon had called him in to her office and asked him what he needed in order to finish the job. Three days and now he was on leave for two weeks—thinking about his future, trying to settle into the 'now' and going quietly out of his mind.

'Who writes these delusional masterpieces anyway?' he asked Trig.

'Psychiatrists.' Trig looked up from the parachute spread out before him, eyes narrowed as he took in Jared's scowl. 'Stop obsessing.'

'I'm not obsessing. I'm disagreeing with the evaluation.'

'You shouldn't *have* the evaluation. No disagreeing with that.'

'Apparently I have an Oedipal complex.'

'Your mother's dead, dude. How can you be in love with her?'

'Could be I'm in love with a ghost. A perfect memory.'

'*Was* she perfect?'

Jared thought back to what little he could remember. His mother's wild curly black hair and the deep blue eyes that both he and his sister Lena had inherited. Her patience with her wayward children and her fierce defence of them when anyone else tried to discipline them.

'Yes.'

'You know that if you *do* have an Oedipal complex you're going to have to bond with your father in order to get over it?'

'Bite me.'

'Okay—not ready.'

'*She* said that the last emotional attachment I made was you.'

'Who said?'

'Rowan Farringdon.'

'Ah.'

'What do you mean, "ah"?'

'Are you ready for that beer? I'm *really* ready for a beer.'

'What do you think of her?'

'Who?'

Jared just looked at him.

Trig abandoned his parachute inspection and headed across the huge open entertaining area towards the kitchen.

He pulled out two beers, twisted the tops off and padded back out to the deck area that Jared had made his own.

'She's the first female section head in thirty years,' Trig said as he passed Jared a beer. 'I think she has connections, ambition, and a mind made for taking people apart and reshaping them to her purpose. That's not a criticism, by the way, it's respect. She's older than you, Jare.'

'So?'

'Oedipus?'

'I am *not* looking for a mother figure. Don't make me shoot you. Lena would *not* be pleased.'

'Neither would I.'

'I asked her to have dinner with me.'

'Bet *that* went down a treat.'

'I almost kissed her.' He was rubbing his hand over his lips just thinking about it. 'Wanted to.'

'You want my thoughts on that?' Trig offered warily.

'Only if you're not going to call me psychologically maladjusted, three kinds of stupid, and pathologically unable to take direction.'

'Or you could just be in need of sex.'

'You think I should have sex with her?'

'No, I think you should have sex with someone else.'

'Who?'

'Has that ever been a problem for you before? What about Bridie?'

'Too nice. I want her to be married by now, with a kid on the ground and one on the way.' He caught Trig staring at him strangely and shrugged. 'It's what she wanted.'

'Simone?'

'Too soft. What if I break her?'

'Simone's brother?'

Jared felt his lips twitch. 'The psych report says I'm heterosexual.'

'Yeah, 'cause we're believing that now.' Trig took a long swig of his beer. 'You said you wanted someone who wouldn't break. Just putting it out there…'

'I want a *woman* who won't break, and I've found one. Gorgeous, whip-smart and powerful. And—if I'm reading her right—interested.'

'Yeah…nothing at all to do with you having information she wants.'

'There is that. Still… Makes for interesting conversation.'

And then his phone beeped. He fished it out of his pocket and looked at the message.

'Trouble?'

'Hopefully. Director Farringdon's coming here bright and early Monday morning. For what reason, she doesn't say.'

'Hnh…' offered Trig after a very long pause.

'Probably something to do with Antonov's last mole that I haven't uncovered yet. Probably nothing to do with sex at all. Still…'

Jared was nothing if not adaptable, and he'd take his opportunities as they came.

'Don't do it, my friend,' Trig told him.

'You keep saying that.'

'Think of the complications.'

'She gets what she wants. I get what I want. There *are* none.'

'What about in the long run? How would it affect your career if you had a relationship with her? How would it affect hers?'

'Not sure I have a career left, to be honest. Not sure I want one.'

'And hers?'

'Guess we'd find out.'

Trig's troubled gaze rested on him. 'Jare, do you *ever*

think about what your short-term decisions might cost people in the long run?'

'All the time. I know I've screwed up. Lena getting wounded under my command and now never being able to have kids of her own. That's on me.'

'No. I don't think that. Lena doesn't think that way either. We were in the wrong place at the wrong time. It happens. And we're all still alive.'

'Then you're talking about the lengths I went to to get Antonov? And the fact that he and two others are now dead? That wasn't my intention.'

Trig grew uncharacteristically silent. 'What happened?' he asked finally.

'I had enough information to bring his entire operation down and I needed one more name for my own satisfaction. In reality I probably had enough dirt on him to bring him down six months ago, but I wanted that one last name so much. And then your wedding invitation landed and I decided that enough was enough. I was leaving—first chance I got. Two days later an old business associate of Antonov's turned up with a new grudge and enough C-4 to blow up a battleship—and I let him do just that while I went and got the kid and the nurse and took off.'

'And your problem with that is...?'

'I wanted revenge and I got it. Not sure I wanted it that way. Antonov wasn't all bad. He was different things to different people. He had a son he loved. A sister he'd sacrificed all contact with to protect. Those other dead men—they had families back in Belarus. They sent money back all the time.'

'They're not dead by *your* hand, Jare.'

'Then why do my hands feel so bloody?'

'I don't know. God complex? You are *not* responsible for all the bad things that happen in this world.'

'But I *am* responsible for my actions, and I should be able to foresee some of the consequences. Isn't that what you're trying to tell me when it comes to my interest in Rowan Farringdon?'

'All I'm saying is talk to the woman first—before embarking on the seduction campaign. Women are easy for you—God knows why.'

'Money, looks, renegade status and genius.'

'Like I said, God knows why. And you do *not* need the downfall of the first female section director in thirty years on your already overburdened conscience.'

'She's smarter than that.'

'How do you know? Will you be reading *her* psych report next?'

'Do you think she has one?'

Jared felt the edges of his lips lift. A small smile, but a smile nonetheless. It was good to finally talk to someone freely. Someone who knew him inside out and didn't hold back.

'Doesn't matter. Even if she does, I'm going to ban Damon from getting it for you.'

'You wouldn't.'

'Oh, but I would.'

'Would what?' asked Lena, stepping from the house onto the deck. ''Cause it sounds vaguely threatening.'

'Your brother wants to read Rowan Farringdon's psych report. Among other things.'

'Seems only fair,' Jared murmured. 'She's read mine.'

'Are you *still* smarting about that idiotic psych report?' she asked, and Jared grinned outright this time.

Injury and near death hadn't softened Lena—they'd

simply made her blunter…and surprisingly more affectionate, he decided as she engulfed him from his shoulders up in a fierce hug.

'Where is it?' she murmured. 'Hand it over. I'm going to barbecue it. By the way, I stopped by the fishing co-op and bought barramundi and king prawns. And because I love you both I'm going to cook them up for dinner. You two can unpack the car, make the salads, pour me some wine and make encouraging remarks about my cooking.'

It was good to be home, Jared thought.

Maybe it would be enough.

Monday morning couldn't come around quickly enough for Jared. He'd swum in Damon's pool and in the surf, and nobly restrained himself from getting the windsurfer out. He'd gone with Lena and Trig to one of their favourite local watering holes on the Saturday night and reacquainted himself with old friends as they'd watched whatever game had been on the big sports screen. Flanked by the two people he trusted most, he'd even managed to relax.

But that had been Saturday. By Sunday afternoon Trig and Lena had retired to their farmhouse, and Jared had been rattling around by himself and trying to *stay* relaxed. He hadn't been sleeping well. He missed the rise and fall of the ocean beneath him. Maybe he needed to investigate yacht ownership.

By Monday morning he'd made enquiries on three oceangoing vessels, and the need to *do* something thrummed through him at a low-level burn.

He hauled himself out of the pool and reached for a towel. His body was still various shades of black and blue, with a few cuts and scrapes besides, but other than that he was in good shape. Antonov had kept his crew fighting fit, and there'd been ocean all around them. Regular diving to examine the hull… Swimming…

Maybe Jared should take up marathon swimming now that he was home.

The doorbell rang and he ditched the towel and headed towards it. He opened it and stepped aside to let Rowan Farringdon in.

'Pretty shirt,' he told her, and it was.

The burnt-orange band of colour across the bottom of it suited her. The rest of it was white, and the inch-wide shoulder straps showed off more body tone than he'd expected from someone who sat in a director's chair. The crisp white trousers she had on rested easy over her rear—not too tight, but not baggy either. *Comfortable.* He hadn't expected this woman to look quite so comfortable in casual clothes.

And still maintain her air of authority.

Her gaze swept the open-plan living area and the pool beyond before returning to him.

Jared offered up a lazy grin by way of reward for her attention. 'Would you like pancakes? I'm having pancakes.'

'Is this a variation on dinner?'

Her voice came at him dry as dust and laced with amusement.

'Could be. But it's also breakfast time, and as a good host I'm offering you some. You've come all this way. It's the least I can do.'

'I've been in Brisbane,' she said. 'You're a detour—not the main destination.'

'I'm crushed.' He led her through to the open-plan

kitchen that backed on to the living area and the pool. 'You take your coffee black, right?'

Her coffee at the farmhouse had been black.

She nodded. 'With one.'

He diligently added sugar to her cup. 'I hope you like Turkish? Lena found it for me in town on Saturday. It's good. I had to promise not to mainline it.'

He lit a flame beneath the skillet and waited for it to get hot. He poured her some coffee and set it in front of her. Added butter to the pan and enjoyed the faint sizzle as he pushed it around with a knife. He added the batter next, before turning back to face her.

'What did you want to see me about?'

'Do you always do two things at once?'

'Keeps me from climbing the walls.'

She smiled at that. 'Say you came across some information that connected a now-deceased illegal arms dealer to a respected worldwide charity organisation…'

'In what capacity?'

'They fed Antonov money and within six months he quadrupled it for them.'

'Did they know who they were dealing with?'

'Does it matter?' She eyed him curiously. 'Do *you* think it matters?'

'Yes. Intent matters. Maybe they didn't know who he was or what he did. Maybe they were naive.'

'The charity's intention was to make money. They succeeded well beyond what any regulated money market could ever do for them. Hard to believe that they thought their investment strategy legitimate, but let's ignore that for a moment. What might Antonov's intention have been?'

'What was the charity?'

'They fund medical research.'

Jared frowned and glanced back to see if the pancake batter in the pan had bubbled up yet. Nope.

'When it came to arms dealing Antonov was a cold-hearted businessman who dealt with the highest bidder and cared nothing for cause,' he offered. 'At first glance no one would mistake him for a philanthropist.'

But Rowan Farringdon would already know that from the reports other people had done on the man. She wanted more. She wanted to know if Jared had ever seen into Antonov's head.

'He was also father to a very sick son. I could see him helping out some research foundation in the hope that their research might some day benefit his kid.'

'They say you played chess with the man?'

Jared nodded.

'Did you win?'

'I grew up with a brother and sisters with genius IQs. They used to play each other and sometimes I'd play the winner. Occasionally I even managed to hold my own. Antonov was bright, but he wasn't that bright. His main asset was his ruthlessness. I gave him a good game and I usually made sure he won. Are you going to shut down the charity?'

'That's not my call. Did you drink with him too? Play catch with his kid?'

'Yes,' Jared muttered roughly. 'I did.'

'Yet you still brought him down?'

It was time to turn the pancakes. 'I let him be brought down by someone else, yes.'

'And the fallout was extreme. Antonov and two others dead. The boy—Celik—fatherless now, and returned to his high-class whore of a mother. New players fighting over Antonov's turf. Tell me, Jared—do you sleep?'

'Do *you*?' He tried to keep his voice low and his temper in check. 'What do you want from me? A confession that I have regrets? Yeah, I do. Would I have gone about things differently if I'd known some of the things that I know now? Yes. But what's done is done and I sleep better for it.'

'I don't think you sleep much at all.'

She was too observant.

'I didn't kill them. That was never my intent. Intent is important.' It was all he had left. 'What's *your* background, Rowan? Why do you sit in a director's chair? What's *your* intent?'

'How about you call me Director?'

'In a workplace situation that requires it, I solemnly swear that I will never call you anything else.'

'You really *are* used to getting your own way, aren't you?'

'Firstborn child,' he murmured. 'It's in my file. What about you? Any brothers or sisters?'

'No. My parents were diplomats—children really didn't fit their career plans, so they made do with one. I was raised by my grandfather. He was an Army general.'

'How'd you get your director's chair?'

'Drive, forward-planning and connections. I decided I wanted to run my own covert operations team when I was fifteen.'

'If I told you that I joined the secret intelligence service with all the forethought of an adrenalin junkie in need of his next fix would you smack me?'

'Yes. Please tell me you planned at least *some* of this?'

Jared grinned at her censure. She was a strategist—no question. *His* skills ran more to being pointed in the right direction and doing what was needed. He'd had no problem with his approach whatsoever at first. Right up until he'd realised that he no longer had complete trust in the people doing the pointing. And then life had got increasingly difficult.

'You *could* smack me. We'll see how we go. I might even like it.'

'The way I read it, you have a certain innate…'

'Charm?'

'Cunning,' she corrected. 'A wariness that stems from your lack of trust in others. And you have no small amount of luck. You're tenacious and a natural-born leader. Corbin has a vacant sub-director's chair. He's put you up for consideration.'

Jared set his coffee down abruptly. 'What are my chances of getting it?'

'Corbin's pushing hard. A few of the other directors have questioned your maturity and your ability to plan ahead. No one's blocked you outright yet. That's down to Corbin's political clout, by the way—not yours. You've done no political manoeuvring whatsoever for over two years.'

'Been a little busy elsewhere…'

'We know.' Rowan watched him steadily. 'Do you want it?'

The pancakes were ready. He fished two plates from the cupboard, loaded hers up and took it to the counter. He pushed the sugar bowl towards her and swiftly quartered a couple of lemons. He added more butter to the pan. More pancake mix.

'I don't know.'

'Where do you see yourself in five years?'

'If I'd known this was a job interview I'd have worn a shirt.'

She let her gaze drop to his chest, but it was hard to tell whether she was admiring his physique or cataloguing the bruises on it.

'You could always put one on now.'

'How *do* you sleep?' he asked abruptly. 'How do you smile when people go down and don't get up and it was your call that put them there?'

'You're talking about your sister getting shot?'

'I'm talking about dead men and belief. How do you know that you're doing the right thing? How do you know when you've chosen the lesser of two evils?'

'Intel helps.'

There was a hint of sorrow in her words that commanded his attention.

'Arrogance helps. You have to *want* to take control and believe that you're the best-equipped person to do so.'

'Maybe I *did* believe that I was the person best equipped to take down Antonov two years ago,' he offered raggedly. 'The one with the most determination. The one with the burning desire to do so. Not sure I believe it now.'

He'd opened up to her this much—he might as well let her see the rest of it.

'I can't settle. I don't sleep. I feel like I'm peeling out of my own skin half the time. I came back for the wedding. I forced things into play so that I could be home in time for that. I've left loose threads that I need to go back and tie up and now you want to put me in a manager's chair? I can't do it. I don't belong in a chair. I'm no manager and I can't stand paperwork. All I want to do is clean up my mess.'

'And how would you do that?'

'I need to know what's happening with Celik—Antonov's kid. I promised him he'd be okay. I need to get to Belarus and put something in play there that *might* lead us to the last of Antonov's moles within ASIS. I need to get to the families of the other two dead men and see how they're situated. I need to finish this so I can sleep.'

'You came back too soon.'

'I had to.'

'You put family first.'

'I always will. You can't be too surprised by that. It's all I've ever done.'

He turned the burner off, took hold of the skillet and tipped the pancakes onto his plate. He sat down opposite where she'd been sitting and reached for the sugar.

He ignored her when she slipped in between him and the corner of the kitchen bench, one elbow on the bench as she studied him intently.

Had she squeezed in between him and another person at a bar, in an effort to get served, he wouldn't have thought anything of her proximity. But there was a lot of room at this breakfast bar and she wasn't currently using any of it.

'What are you doing?' he asked warily.

'May I try something?'

'I don't know whether to say yes or no.'

She reached out and slid the back of her hand up his cheek and towards his temple…a soft caress that made his breath hitch and his body stiffen against the utter pleasure of it. Her hand didn't stop there and soon her fingers were in his hair, scraping gently across his scalp, making his eyes close and his body tremble.

'You're touch-starved.'

Her whisky voice rippled across his senses.

'We see it sometimes in those who've held themselves apart, those who've gone too deeply undercover for too long. I thought I saw a hint of it the other day in your sister's kitchen, and then again in my office. You weren't looking for it. You thought yourself attracted to *me*.'

'I *am* attracted to you. How much more obvious do you want me to be?'

He caught her wrist, then deliberately brought her hand back to the counter before releasing her. He wasn't going to act the Neanderthal the way he had the other day. He just wasn't.

'Move over,' she said, and reached across the bench for her plate of pancakes and her utensils.

When she sat down beside him she let her lower leg rest against his, pinching his footrest instead of using hers.

'Touch doesn't always have to be sexual. Sometimes it's about comfort and connection.'

'Are you *mentoring* me?'

'You did say I could. Are you objecting?'

'Yes,' he said firmly, and glared when she patted him on the forearm. 'And don't mother me either. Don't need one—don't want one. Don't call *me* Oedipus.'

She smiled like a Madonna. 'I challenge you to stay in casual body contact with me for five minutes and see if it relaxes you any. If it works we'll get you a puppy.'

'Don't want a puppy, Ro.' He gave her his full wattage smile. 'I want a *girl*.'

'And I thought you wanted *me*. How are your ribs?'

'Better.'

'The doctor said it would take weeks for them to fully heal.'

'Almost better.'

'It's probably too soon for you to be playing contact sport as a way of encountering touch. There's massage…?'

Her leg was already sliding against his as he moved his own leg around. 'The frustration would kill me.'

'Self-massage beforehand?'

'Wouldn't help.'

'Maybe you could take dance classes? Start with a waltz…finish at the tango?'

'No partner.'

'The dance teacher would be your partner.'

'You're really serious about this touch thing, aren't you?'

'Are you feeling more relaxed than you were a minute ago?'

Surprisingly, he was.

'Might not be about touch, though. Might be proximity to *you*. You could stay the night. There could be dinner out on the deck. A swim this afternoon. I could teach you how to kite surf.'

He wasn't allowed to, on account of his ribs, but that wouldn't stop him teaching someone else.

'Wouldn't I have to learn how to surf first?'

'Oh, Ro… *No*. You don't surf? Do you know what this means?'

'That we may not be soul mates after all?'

'It means you're missing out on one of life's great pleasures. Now I *have* to teach you how to surf.'

'You mean right after you teach me how to swim?'

For a moment he thought she was serious, and then she smiled and he knew she was playing him. 'You can swim. The General would have made sure of it.'

She laughed at that. 'And then there was canoeing and sailing—diving and the rest. I swear that man should have joined the Navy, not the Army.'

He liked hearing those kinds of things from her, liked having her around.

'Can you stay? We *could* swim or surf—the offer's there. You *could* stay the night—there's plenty of bedrooms. We *could* go out to dinner. There could be fresh seafood and bright stars in the sky. A playful breeze. There could be body contact and relaxation. I'm all for it.'

'My flight leaves at midday. This is a work-day for me.'

'There's always next weekend. You could come back.'

Her leg rocked gently against his. 'You're very tempting. You already know this, so it's not as if I'm telling you anything new. But you're not in a good place right now, and I'm trying to figure out what I *need* to do for you in a work capacity and what I *might* be able to offer you in a private one. The answer to that second question being that if I know what's good for me I'll offer you nothing.'

'We could try friendship?' he offered. 'Something simple. I'd like simple.'

'You'd need to stop hitting on me. And—given that I have at least *some* self-awareness—I'd need to stop flirting with you too.'

Rowan smiled ruefully and turned her attention to the eating of her pancakes. They ate in companionable silence, and by the time Rowan had finished her pancakes and drunk her coffee Jared was feeling more at ease.

'Get a massage,' she told him as she stood to leave. 'Go hug people. Use the beach and concentrate on the physical sensation of the waves breaking over you and the sun on your skin. Hold your hand over your heart and breathe. Concentrate on sensory details when you want to give your brain a rest.'

'You're giving me coping mechanisms for *anxiety*?'

'You asked me how I cope with some of the decisions I've had to make over the years. I'm telling you what has helped me.'

'Sex.'

Jared rubbed his hand across the back of his neck and tried to explain his thought processes before Rowan decided that he was hitting on her again.

'Trig said I needed sex.'

'It's not a bad idea—provided that your partner knows what you're having sex for.'

'I'm pretty sure that telling someone I'm touch-starved and over-anxious and therefore need to have sex isn't going to fly.'

'Oh, I don't know… With *your* face and body?' She leaned across the counter for her black leather satchel. 'It might.'

'Are you flirting again?'

'I hope not.' She stood up and slung the satchel over her shoulder. 'Time for me to go.'

'Yeah.' He didn't want her to go. 'Do you need any more on Antonov?'

'No. That wasn't the main reason I came here and you know it. I wanted to check up on you—see how you were tracking. I'm supposed to be gaining your trust, and that's hard to do when you're nowhere in my vicinity. I was also very curious as to whether you want that sub-director's chair.'

'Director—' He knew she'd notice the name-change. He hoped she knew that he was replying to the chair now and not just to her. 'I don't want a promotion. I can't think about that right now. If you want me to do what I do best, cancel my leave and get me to Belarus. Let me clean up my mess.'

She looked at him hard.

He waited.

Finally, she nodded. 'Belarus it is, then.'

'When?'

'Any objection to coming with me now?'

'None at all.'

'In that case pack what you need and put on a shirt.'

Jared shot her a brilliant smile as he stood to do her bidding. Or his bidding. Either way, he thoroughly approved of the direction this beautiful friendship was going in.

'Hey, Ro? The touch thing? I think it's working.'

'Nothing at all to do with getting your own way?'

'Oh, you noticed that?'

She spared him a very level glance. 'I'm setting you loose in Belarus for two reasons. One: I want that final head to roll and I have my own thoughts as to who it is—I just don't quite have enough to nail him yet, and with your help maybe we'll get there. Two: you're not recuperating here in your brother's beach house...you're drowning, and I have rope that might save you. I suggest you grab it.'

CHAPTER SIX

BY THE TIME they touched down in the capital Rowan had done a whole lot of touching, brushing against and just plain standing close to Jared West, and the extended contact was beginning to take a toll on her senses. She liked the smell of him and the feel of him.

Everyone liked the sight of him. He'd changed into a business suit and he wore it to perfection. It gave him an air of authority and added a couple more years to his thirty. His wristwatch signalled the kind of wealth that got handed down from generation to generation. His grandfather, according to the records, had made a fortune in shipping, and his father had taken it into the investment banking arena and quadrupled it. Between Jared, his siblings and his elders, they had property on every continent and in most major cities.

For Jared to choose working for secret intelligence over all the other options available to him had been an unusual move. For him not to want to advance through the ranks now was more unusual still. She didn't know what drove him—beyond family loyalty and wanting to clean up his mess.

'Jared?' she said as they stepped from the airport terminal and headed towards a waiting car. 'Don't make me regret my belief in you.'

He glanced her way, his gaze strangely searching. 'What is it about me that you believe in?'

'I believe that you want to see this through.' She nodded to Jeffers, her driver, who had opened the door as she approached, sparing only a glance for Jared.

Jared settled in beside her. Jeffers handed her a tablet and she took it and opened up her information stream. Jared didn't ask anything else. He let her get on with it and looked out of the window, deep in his own thoughts.

It wasn't until they were back in the corridors of Section that he spoke again. 'How soon can I leave?'

'I'll need to bring you into my section and under my jurisdiction first. At the moment you're Corbin's.'

'Will Corbin be a problem?'

'We're about to find out.'

They'd reached her office and Sam looked up, her cool gaze encompassing them both.

'Director. Agent West.'

'Mr West needs to book a flight to wherever it is he's going. I'll leave him with you.'

But Jared followed her to her door instead of taking his cue. 'Don't I get to listen in on your courtesy call?'

'No. Try not to annoy Sam too much, Mr West. She's perfectly capable of sending you to Belarus via Antarctica.'

'I'll keep that in mind,' he murmured.

She smiled encouragingly and shut the door on him with no little satisfaction. Back in her domain, back in control, and out of range of that killer smile and perfect body. He was hard on the senses, Jared West. Hard on the mind.

She wasn't game to examine her confidence.

* * *

Rowan's conversation with George Corbin didn't begin well.

'You can't have him,' he said curtly when she put her request to him. 'He's on medical leave.'

'He's back, he's bored, and I need him for a job.'

'Consulting?'

'Fieldwork.' She knew damn well that her decision to send Jared back into the field wasn't going to go down a treat. No need to mention that the job was Antonov-related.

'You're crazier than I thought.'

'Will you release him or not? He doesn't want your sub-director's chair, by the way.'

'Maybe I never expected him to take it in the first place.'

She could hear the older director's exasperation, loud and clear.

'Maybe all I'm trying to do is get him looking towards a future in which Antonov's reach *isn't* his entire focus. Get him thinking about how to come out of this current situation with his career intact. Maybe I simply don't like watching one of our best and brightest break.'

'He won't break. He'll do what's asked of him.'

'Says who? Him? Or you? He's not physically fit. He's not mentally ready. What makes you think that if you send him out now he'll even return? What makes you think he won't end up in pieces?'

'He'll come back when he's due back—and it won't be in a body bag.' She could picture Corbin's cold grey eyes and his tightly drawn lips. 'Do I need to call in favours?'

'I don't *owe* you any favours.'

'In that case I'll owe *you*.'

She could practically hear the older man calculating what he might demand of her. Nothing good.

Eventually he spoke again. 'You can have him—but my objections are going on record.'

'Thanks, George. That's exactly what I wanted to hear.'

Corbin hung up.

Rowan put the phone down, closed her eyes, and banged her head against the padded leather headrest of her chair a couple of times.

That had been so *not* what she'd wanted to hear.

If Jared didn't come through with the name of that final mole she was screwed.

Several hours later Rowan had managed to wade her way through most of her work for the day. Tomorrow's schedule was in place, Sam was finishing up, and the only memo sheet left on her desk was the one regarding Jared's impending travel arrangements.

He was booked to go via Warsaw with his first flight leaving at four-forty a.m. He was scheduled to return four days after he got there. Six days in total—not nearly long enough for him to pay his respects to two dead men's families, check on a kid in the Netherlands, and go after the name of Antonov's final mole. His arrangements were flawed from the beginning.

Not a good start.

'Agent West wanted to know what time you usually leave the office,' Sam said as she shut down her computer and secured her desk drawers with the thoroughness with which one might secure a safe.

'What did you tell him?'

'She said I should be able to catch you about now.'

The office door was open. How Jared had managed to appear framed in it without either her or Sam hearing him was a testament to how quietly he could move.

She nodded to him, eyeing the carry-bag draped over his shoulder and the white plastic shopping bag that dangled from one hand. The plastic bag smelled strongly of chilli, basil, lemongrass and curry.

'You told her I'd be back with food, right?' he asked Sam.

'I was just about to mention it.' Sam turned her blandest gaze on Rowan. 'I didn't say you'd eat it.'

'Is this a variation on *Will you have dinner with me?*' Rowan asked him.

'Or I can eat and you can watch,' he offered with a sinner's smile. 'I'm hungry.'

'Apparently you're also very fragile—I've been hearing that all day. This had better not be your version of the Last Supper.'

'If it was I'd have chosen the lobster instead of the duck.'

Not for a second did he let her see whether her words had got to him. And then his gaze skidded to her mouth and hers went to his for more than a count of three.

Damn. Rowan dragged her gaze back to the rest of his face and motioned him into her office.

'See you in the morning, Sam.'

Sam nodded and left without another word. Jared walked past Rowan and headed straight over to the panelled bookcase that doubled as a door that led through to her private apartment. He knew how to open it and didn't wait to be invited inside—just strode on through.

Perhaps he expected her to follow.

Warily, she did.

Rowan didn't use the apartment often. She kept a few changes of clothes there, a few emergency toiletries in the bathroom cupboard. Sometimes she ate there. But not often.

'You know the layout of my office and you know my favourite food. What else do you know?' she asked as she leaned against the doorframe and watched him make himself at home.

'Have you eaten since you ate my pancakes this morning?'

She hadn't.

'That's what I thought.'

He found plates in the cupboard and cutlery in the drawer. He fished napkins from the bag and she let him, more focused on his economy of movement in such a small kitchenette space than on his words.

'I bought a boat today.'

'What kind of boat?'

'An oceangoing yacht.'

'Do you miss Antonov's yacht?'

'That was a floating fortress, not a yacht. I don't miss it specifically. I *do* miss being at sea.'

'You work in Canberra. How often are you going to use this yacht?'

'Not as often as I'd like, but I won't be the only one using it. Lena went halves on it with me.'

'That must be nice.'

She didn't mean for him to stop serving up the food— heaven forbid—but he paused long enough to slide her an enquiring glance.

'Having siblings to share things with,' she elaborated. 'Do you have a favourite sibling?'

'Lena's closest to me in age. Closest to me overall.'

And Lena had just married Jared's best friend.

'Lena followed you and Adrian Sinclair into the service. You made a good, reliable team, the three of you. You led, and mostly they followed. And then Lena got shot while the three of you were checking out an abandoned biological weapons factory in East Timor.'

Jared's lips tightened.

'Adrian stayed to look after her. You, on the other hand, went rogue, trying to pin down who was responsible for hurting your sister.'

'I had a handler. I didn't go rogue. Serrin knew what I was doing.'

'I've read Serrin's notes,' she countered mildly. 'Frankly, they made me wonder who was running who.'

'Still not rogue. I worked within the framework that was there.'

He handed her a plate piled high with red curry duck, plain rice and Asian greens.

'Where's the wine?' she asked.

'You don't drink.' He said it with utter confidence.

'We really *are* going to have to stop letting your brother use our database as his personal information library.'

Jared smiled and shoved a forkful of food into his mouth. Rowan looked at her plate and headed for the little table in the room. She walked over to it, pulled out a chair and kicked another one out for him. He joined her moments later.

Corbin's words of warning slid insidiously through her mind. *Don't bury him. Don't send this man to his death.*

She didn't want to. 'What's in Belarus?'

'Churches, city squares, a fine fear of the Motherland and a man Antonov wanted to impress.'

'A man Antonov wanted to *impress*?' The only people she could think of who might fit that particular criteria would be hellishly hard to access. Rebel leaders and legitimate ones. People of power. 'Does this man have a name?'

'Ro, you haven't even tried your duck. It's really good.'

'Do you know how to find him?'

'Yes.'

'And then what?'

'I think he knows who Antonov's main mole within Section is.'

'Assuming you're right, you still have to get that information out of him.'

Jared said nothing.

'Are you going to bring him in?'

'Wasn't planning on it.'

'It's an option.'

'Given who he is, it's really not.'

Something to chew on… 'Does your sister know that you're going back out there? Does Sinclair?'

'No.' Jared kept right on eating.

Rowan nudged his foot with hers. 'Will you tell them before you go?'

'Wouldn't want to worry them.'

'Withholding your whereabouts from them isn't going to make them worry any *less*. I thought you'd have learned that lesson by now?'

Jared scowled. 'I'll phone them from the airport. Satisfied?'

'Beats having Sinclair and your sister contacting *me*

for your whereabouts. I'm all for delegating my excess workload. You're on record for this trip, by the way. Check your inbox. You're liaising with a new informant on my behalf.'

Jared's scowl had morphed into something a whole lot more thoughtful. Rowan studied his face—the refined masculine beauty of it, the cuts and bruises that hadn't quite faded from it. She was risking her neck for this man and she still didn't really know why.

Take a deep ops agent, fresh from two years in the field, driven by a personal vendetta and deep feelings of failure and responsibility, one who had a dislike of authority and a bad case of alienation and expect him to be a team player?

No. A team player he wasn't.

The best Rowan could do was give him the space he needed to get the job done and hope that there were pieces of him to pick up afterwards.

'Jared, are you up to this?'

'Yes.'

She wanted to believe him.

'Yes,' he repeated. 'I know you've probably had to convince, connive and bury my psych report in order to get me back out there this fast, but I won't let you down. Trust me.'

She nodded—because it was a more positive response than telling him to please stay alive.

She took a couple of mouthfuls of the curry. 'The duck *is* good.'

'Yeah.'

They finished the rest of their meal in silence. It wasn't a companionable silence—more like a heavy, expectant waiting. Jared cleaned up. Rowan helped. His shoulder brushed against hers—the chambray of his shirt soft and well-worn against the bare skin of her shoulder—and her nipples pebbled tightly beneath her bra. She had a jacket somewhere. Wouldn't hurt to put it on and get the hell gone from here before the mind-melting awareness between them turned into hot, sweaty sex.

'If I was ten years older would you take my attraction to you more seriously?' he asked.

So much for ignoring the elephant in the room.

'It's not the age difference.' *Nothing but the truth.* 'Given your experience with life, loss and the demands of intelligence work, you'd be a good match for me. Your body in its prime would just be a bonus.'

'Is there someone else in your life?'

'No.' *Not for years.*

'Who *do* you get intimate with?'

'Since the director's chair? No one.'

'Well, that can't be healthy. How long do you plan on *keeping* the chair?'

'It's hard to say. It was my end-game. I got here a little sooner than expected. Now I'm regrouping. Starting to plan ahead.'

Next thing she knew she'd be revealing that sometimes she questioned what had driven her to this and whether the power she now wielded had been worth the sacrifice. The gruelling hours and the responsibility. Always having to watch her back on account of the power games people played. She could count on one hand the number of people she truly trusted.

Even Jared trusted more people than she did.

'You could set your sights on the top job,' he said. 'Run the division.'

'I could. That's likely to depend on the mistakes I

make in this job and the never-ending politics. Are you going to be a mistake on my résumé?'

'No.' He held her gaze. 'That's not the plan.'

'Then what *is* the plan? You come in here this evening, bearing food—'

'People eat in this building all the time.'

'Yes, in the twenty-four-hour cafeteria.'

'Never seen a director eating in there yet. You could have asked me and my duck to leave.'

'And I will—but not before you give me the name of your informant.'

'And what will you give me in return?'

'Permission to leave the room *and* the country.'

'I want a kiss.'

Nothing but challenge in the rough purr of his voice and speculation in his eyes.

'Because *that's* not going to undermine my authority at all?' she offered dryly.

'You're a little hung up on authority, Ro.'

'It comes with the territory.'

'Last chance,' he offered. 'You want a name; I want a kiss. Think of it as a trust-building exercise.'

'Or blackmail?'

'A freely given exchange,' he countered smoothly.

'If you don't return—if you crash and burn or simply decide that your attention is needed elsewhere—my head is going to roll unless I have something to bargain with. I'm trusting you to do your job, and I have precious little reason for doing so other than gut instinct. I want the name of your informant and I want you back here in six days—free of all Antonov baggage, clear-headed and fit to work.'

'*Then* do I get my kiss?'

'Then you gain my trust—and, for what it's worth, my respect. Finish the job, Jared. And then we'll talk relationships and sex.'

CHAPTER SEVEN

JARED STARTED WITH money for the families first. Local currency and plenty of it. Their dead loved one had had an insurance policy, courtesy of their employer, he told the head of each family. Blood money—nothing more than a Band-Aid applied to his conscience and a couple of years' financial security for the families—but he had to believe that it would help. Money always helped—stained red or not.

He went after Yegor Veselov next, who was in Singapore. It took him another day to get to him and extract the information he required, and by then he'd missed his scheduled flight back to Australia.

His new director was *not* going to be impressed.

He rang Sam instead. 'Tell her I missed my flight.'

'Oh, no. You can tell her yourself.'

He guessed he didn't have to identify himself.

There was a click, two rings, and he almost hung up—like a kid on a prank call. Instead he waited.

'Jared?' his director offered curtly. 'This better be good.'

He gave her the name of another director and smiled mirthlessly when the first words out of her mouth were 'I knew it.'

'You're sexy when you're smug.'

'Does that line *ever* work for you?'

'I've never used it before. It's a first.'

'In that case I'll attempt to feel flattered. Is our informative friend in travelling shape? Can you bring him in to testify against our man?'

'Doesn't seem wise. He's currently dining with an Eastern Bloc president. Or aren't we caring about that?'

'I guess we're caring,' she said. 'So, have you tied up all your other loose ends?'

'I still need to check on the kid. I need another couple of days.'

'No, you need to prove yourself reliable and be back here when you said you would be. That's non-negotiable.'

'Even though I've given you a name?'

'That name is going to need your weight behind it. Is there any reason you need to see this kid in the flesh?' she countered flatly.

Besides wanting to see Celik for himself and gauge the child's wellbeing...?

'He's being monitored by the Dutch authorities,' she offered next. 'Check up on him that way, and if you're still not satisfied I'll send you to the Netherlands to see him—no question.'

'I'm already halfway there.'

'I'm sending you the contact details for the Dutch who are monitoring him. Call them. And then, in the interest of your future career and my current one, get back here.'

'Is that an order?'

'You don't take orders, so let me put it another way. You asked for my co-operation and trust and I gave them to you. How about you goddamn *earn* it?'

* * *

Jared walked with new purpose and confidence. He wasn't fixed, by any means—he still slept far less than any man should, and indecision still plagued him—but there was no denying that a weight had lifted from his shoulders now that he'd finally finished what he set out to do. Expose the rot in the counter-intelligence organisation he worked for—all the way back to the roots. Maybe now he could rest and get his life back. Figure out what it was he wanted now.

Apart from that kiss.

Director Rowan Farringdon sat at her desk and watched him approach, her eyes sharp and assessing. Probably looking for signs of weakness or fatigue, injury or distress. It didn't sit well with him that she was most likely sitting there trying to assess his needs. On the one hand he drew comfort from her concern. On the other hand it made him feel somehow…*less*.

Less worthy, maybe.

Less capable than he was.

'I'm back,' he said by way of greeting. 'What did you do with the information I gave you?'

'I sent it to the top.'

'Will they be able to get rid of him? With your information and mine, is it enough?'

'I put together a solid case. I believe it'll be enough. Have you had any sleep?'

'I slept on the plane.' More or less. Mostly less.

'In that case you're wanted upstairs. Management wants a word.'

'That's a level of management I've never been introduced to. Any tips?'

'Yes. Try to impress them.'

She stood and came around her big glossy table, crossed the room to where he was standing with his feet slightly apart and his hands behind his back. She stood a good head shorter than him, even in shoes with medium heels. Today she wore a steel-grey dress with a geometrical pattern on the front in pewter and bronze. Professional and classy. Beautiful lean muscles and some very nice curves.

He wanted very badly to have earned the trust she'd placed in him.

He thought he might have.

He wanted very badly to trust that she'd made the right call when it came to him not going to check on the kid.

'Jared,' she murmured. 'My face is up here.'

'I know.' He got there eventually and smiled—because he wanted to.

'Thank you for coming back on time and in one piece,' she said. 'I'm impressed.'

'Did you doubt me?'

'Yes.'

And then she stepped up into his space, slid her hand around his neck and fitted her lips to his.

It was a quiet kiss—neither tentative nor bold. A very welcome kiss. He tried not to frighten her, tried not to let his hunger show… Except that one second he had his desire under control and his hands behind his back and the next moment he had his hands either side of her face and his longing could no longer be denied.

He coaxed her mouth open and she responded with an intrusion both accomplished and welcome. She tasted of passion and perfection and he groaned his pleasure, for it was a taste he hadn't known he craved until this moment.

He tilted his head and deepened the kiss, unleashed his hunger for her just a little bit and felt her match it.

And, *oh*, the intensity she brought to everything she did—to the feeding of her need and his. He loved it.

Testing her, he unleashed a little more, and her eyes swept closed even as her mouth opened greedily. Careful, considered exploration turned into surrender after that as he offered up *his* kind of hunger—the kind with a hard and dangerous edge. *His* brand of possession—desperate and all-encompassing. And Ro…Rowan Farringdon…his director…was right there with him.

Revelling.

As if she'd been made for him.

He had her backed against the table moments later, because all he could think was that there was so much more of her to explore and he wanted his mouth on every last bit of it—no self-restraint left. Only then did she wrench her mouth from his with a gasp and put her hand to his chest to stop him.

Not that it stopped the tremor that ripped through him.

'Are you eating with anyone this evening?' he muttered roughly.

'I'm working late.'

'After that?'

'What? No offer to bring dinner here?'

'I want you gone from this place.'

He wanted equal footing and he wouldn't get it here.

'I want to take you back at my place, or the beach house—anywhere that's private. I want to be in you, over you, under you, touching you for a good long while, and I want to make good on any promises I made to you that first night at my sister's wedding.'

A slow smile lit her eyes at that. 'You never made any.'

'Make 'em up.'

Her mouth joined the smiling caper then—a generous curve that he desperately needed to explore some more.

'You're wanted upstairs,' she murmured. 'I'll be finished here by ten p.m. and I'll be back at six tomorrow morning. I'll need food at some point, and I'll need a bed to sleep in. You can pick me up at five past ten from the steps outside the entrance to the building.'

'You don't mind people here knowing who you're going home with?'

'It'll be a problem, yes. How about we let the others choke on it?'

'Dangerous…' He liked it.

'Nothing I can't handle.'

'Have they give you permission to seduce me?'

'They've given me permission to use whatever means necessary to gain your trust and co-operation. Not that I need to sleep with you to do that. Let's not mistake work for willingness.'

'*Are* you willing, Ro?'

'What do you think?'

He waited until he'd reached the door before looking back. She was still leaning against the desk, still wholly focused on him. He wondered if his lips looked as kiss-blown as hers.

'How many hours of sleep do you need?'

She held his gaze and the smile she sent him was full of promise.

'In any one night? Six.'

Jared was used to men in suits looking him over and not liking what they saw. He was used to them seeing him as either a threat or a weapon to be used against others. He usually enjoyed a certain measure of respect—and when he'd been in Antonov's service fear. Lust—he got that too.

Utter indifference was new to him.

The man standing behind the desk was reptilian— cold and imposing to look at. Pale grey eyes and grey- ing black hair…that rare mix of colour that came out of nowhere and stayed in the mind like a thorn. He was in his fifties, at a guess. Big-bodied, well-honed and pow- erful. Imposing.

'You hand me the head of one of my directors on a plate and yet you've no ambition to succeed him?'

The man's voice matched his looks. Cold. Precise.

'You don't like the rules so you either bend them or outright break them. You've no wish to remake them, apparently, and you're about to start screwing one of my best directors. Tell me, West, what would *you* do with you?'

'Probably move me on.'

'To where, exactly?'

'A place where section rules don't apply.'

'Why would you even think such a place exists?'

'They always exist.'

The head of the service smiled mirthlessly. 'If you could put together a team for this place where normal rules don't apply, who would you choose?'

'Adrian Sinclair and my sister Lena.'

'Sinclair I approve of. But your sister's performance record is unremarkable and her injuries are extensive. What would you do with her?'

The man had no idea of Lena's determination or her fierce loyalty to family.

Jared didn't bother explaining it to him—just ran through the rest of his list. 'My brother, Damon. My sister Poppy.'

'You've no problem with leading them into danger? Your psych report suggests otherwise.'

'They'd follow me there regardless. May as well make it easier on them.'

'Who else?'

'That's it.'

'Not Rowan Farringdon?'

'She'd limit me. Rein me in.'

'If you let her, yes.'

'Not really my thing.'

'You were doing well until then.'

'You need to find someone who cares.' *May as well come clean.* 'I want Antonov's last mole gone and then I really don't know what I want. I don't like being used, lied to, and finding myself on my own when I come in from fieldwork that *you* authorised.'

Not for a second did the older man look contrite.

'Should you agree to head up this team you'll report directly either to me or to the woman whose desk you passed on the way into this office.'

'Your secretary?'

'She's not a secretary.'

'Then what is she, exactly?'

'My confidante. My partner in all things. My conscience, at times, as I am hers. Vera stays in the outer office because she says it keeps her more connected to section politics than she would be if she held equal title to me. Her choice, and I respect her for it. Vulnerability and accessibility are powerful weapons.'

Not what he'd been expecting—and the older man knew it.

'Every system can be exploited, Mr West. Patriarchy, especially.'

Now *there* was an argument. He wondered what the woman he'd just kissed would think of it. Whether the lesser status would satisfy her. He didn't think so, frankly.

'How would you expect me to trust you *or* your associate? How would I know that the information you'd be feeding me was good?'

'You'd get your team to double-check it. I would have a checking mechanism in place as well. Everyone wins.' The older man's cold grey eyes narrowed. 'I expect you to put together a black ops crew and run them in a manner that will get the job done—*any* job done. You're being groomed, Mr West, for this chair, no less—in about ten years' time, all going well, it will be yours. If you're not inclined towards this outcome you may tender your resignation from the department on your way out.'

'Do I get time to think about it?'

'If you need time to think about it you're not the right man for the job.'

Jared smiled grimly. 'I don't believe that.'

'Tell me, Mr West, do you question *everything*?'

'Do *you*?'

This time he won from the man a smile that might have been genuine.

'If you have a job for me in the here and now I'll look at the brief,' Jared told him. 'I'll make the acquaintance of your partner. I'll approach the people I trust and see if they're willing to go where I lead. And I will let you know, after that, whether I can be what you need.'

Jared didn't consider his stance out of line, considering what the older man was asking of him. And if it was—well, maybe it *was* time to leave.

CHAPTER EIGHT

HE WAS WAITING for her when she stepped from the building and started down the stairs to the footpath. Rowan quickened her step and tried to ignore the acceleration of her heartbeat. His car was sleek, black, expensive, and parked in a no standing zone—and he leaned against the gleaming paintwork as if he had all the time in the world.

He wore battered jeans, a shirt with a collar and a black leather jacket, and he'd look like every muscled guy she'd ever seen in the movies but for the sheer beauty of his face and the fierce intelligence in those midnight-blue eyes. Two of his younger siblings had genius IQs. Jared had been tested too, in his younger years, and those tests had been re-analysed again recently. There was some reason to believe that Jared had screwed those tests up deliberately.

Brains, brawn, an ingrained disrespect for authority, a taste for revenge and utter loyalty to his family. As a director, Rowan had no idea how to handle him. As a woman she had an unhealthy desire to get under his skin and become important to him in ways they'd both regret.

Not exactly a comfortable headspace to be in.

He opened the car door for her as she approached, and she slid him a careless smile and got in.

'Where are we going?' she asked when he took the driver's seat.

'Some place nice.'

'Some place neutral?'

'My father keeps an apartment here for family use. I haven't been in it for over two years and I probably haven't stayed there for close to five years. Is that neutral enough for you?'

'I guess we'll see.' She gave tacit agreement to the plan. 'How far away is it?'

'It's in a hotel complex near here. There are several restaurants to choose from—or, if you prefer, Room Service. You'll have immediate access to other people should you decide to leave the privacy of the apartment. There's a concierge who can call you a taxi if you need one.'

'Am I going to need one?'

'I don't know. Either way, you'll have a swift and easy exit available.'

'Thank you.'

She leaned back against the leather seat and closed her eyes. Her last meeting of the day had been difficult. Jockeying with other section heads for project priority was always taxing. When it came to having dinner with Jared, she'd barely had time to think beyond the fact that she'd agreed to it. That he'd gone ahead and taken the time to plan the evening carefully, with both her physical and emotional comfort in mind, was a very welcome bonus.

'How did your meeting with the management go?'

'It threw up some…unexpected career opportunities.'

He could have said more but he lapsed into silence

and Rowan didn't push him. Sharing information didn't come easily to this man. Trust had to be built slowly.

She opened her eyes and looked in his direction, instantly captivated by the play of shadows across the hard lines of his face and those perfectly formed lips. He was so very beautiful to look at. She doubted she'd ever tire of doing so.

'I patted a puppy this afternoon,' he offered next, with a wry smile in her direction. 'It wasn't *my* puppy, mind, but I figured it counted as far as taking your advice was concerned. Do *you* have any pets, Ro?'

'My grandfather has a tortoise. Apparently I'll inherit.'

He laughed—and *there* was a sound to make a woman sit up and take notice, for it was a good laugh. Rich and rolling. Infectious.

The hotel he took her to looked unimposing from the outside—nothing more than a single set of oversized wooden doors with a black-suited doorman attending them—but the inside was a different matter altogether. Anyone would be able to see this place was on the seven-star side of exclusive the minute they stepped through the doors. Assuming you were allowed through the doors at all.

Jared had to hand the doorman a plastic swipe card and then face a camera and be photo-IDd. Rowan had to be IDd as well, for this hotel clearly took the security of their guests and visitors extremely seriously.

'Your family keeps an apartment here and no one uses it?' she asked as they stepped into a gilt-edged lift with bronze handrails and mirrors. The kind of lift a princess or a president might be acquainted with.

'My grandfather bought it. My father keeps it mainly for sentimental reasons, I think. Occasionally he uses it to impress. Doesn't mean he doesn't profit from it. We have an agreement with the hotel whereby they have the authority to put guests in the suite when we're not using it.'

The apartment he took her to was a three-bedroom penthouse, complete with a ten-person dining table, a bar, and an exquisitely furnished lounge area. It was the kind of suite that foreign dignitaries and heads of state stayed in. It was the kind of hotel that afforded its guests several extra layers of security.

'This do?' Jared asked as he shut the door behind them.

'Yes!' Opulence, privacy, and service at their fingertips. 'You knew it would impress.'

'No. I just hoped it would fit our needs. I have no idea what would impress you.'

'Loyalty. Intelligence. Self-awareness. I'm impressed.'

For a fleeting moment he looked boyishly pleased, and then he shrugged and added a few more words to the mix. 'Vengeful, destructive, inaccessible...'

'Trifles,' she said. 'You'll grow out of it.'

He laughed at her words, his eyes warm and his expression boyishly unguarded. 'We'll see.' He crossed to the bar. 'What can I get you to drink?'

'Cool, clear, bubble-infested water.'

'Do you *ever* drink alcohol?'

'Occasionally. I don't dislike it. It's more a matter of being permanently on call.'

'That's a strong service ethic you have there, Ro.'

Maybe he meant it as a criticism—she didn't know. 'Plenty of people have one.'

He nodded and handed her the room service menu, then tucked in shoulder to shoulder with her while she read it. She didn't push him away. He felt good and smelled better, the faintly woodsy tang of his aftershave teasing her senses.

'Veal for me,' she decided after careful perusal. 'With the creamy fennel sauce and greens—and I absolutely *do* want the wattle-seed and bush honey *crème brûlée* afterwards.'

'I'm having the rib-eye,' he said. 'With fries, cracked pepper, salad to make it look healthy, and a beer to wash it down with. I'm a simple soul. And I'm not on call.'

He picked up the hotel phone and put the order through.

'Someone's coming to sort out the dining area and bring bread and tapas for us,' he offered when he'd finished.

'Good service.'

'Always is.'

She cocked her head to one side. 'You're used to this level of wealth?'

'I don't need it,' he said with a shrug. 'I can exist on a lot less. But, yes. I was born into wealth. I've never wanted for playthings. What about you?'

'I'm used to less.'

He crossed to the entertainment console and moments later the soft strains of a well-played acoustic guitar filled the room. A little bit Spanish…a little bit alternative.

'Your choice?' she asked.

'Probably Damon's—although I recognise who's playing. Sounds of my youth.'

'Do those youthful memories relax you? The ones you had before ASIS?'

'Yes. There are good memories there. My teenage

years were good ones. I thought myself invincible and thought that the world revolved around my every whim. Because it did.'

'See? Told you—you'll grow out of things.'

This man could have done anything. Been anything. Yet here he was.

'Why did you join ASIS?'

'I think I was looking for a cause. A way to combine adrenalin-junked-up dangerous activities with righteousness.'

'What did your father say to that decision?'

'Nothing.' Jared shrugged. 'It's not that we don't get on. We just never saw much of him after my mother's death. Damon and Poppy got the worst end of that stick. They barely know the man at all.'

'Do they care?'

Jared shrugged. 'Can't speak for them, but I like to hope that even if our father wasn't around much while they were growing up they didn't miss out on having family who loved and cared for them. Lena's good at binding people together. Love, concern, support—just being there for people in the day-to-day. She's bossy as all hell, mind—and so was I. But the four of us kids held together as a family. We still hold, even though we're scattered across the globe.'

'I'm glad you have them.'

'Trig's a part of the family too. I've been thinking about something he said the other day. A question he asked me. You and me…if we get together…how will that affect your career? Are you looking to me to enhance it?'

He crossed to the bar, poured himself a Scotch and stared down at it, frowning.

'Because I have to tell you, Ro, that I'm considering finishing up with special intelligence altogether—so if you have some notion that you and I could team up at some point…be some kind of power couple within the organisation…I'm not on board with it.'

It had been a long time since someone had managed to shock her so thoroughly, and it must have shown on her face because Jared suddenly grinned.

'A *power couple*?' she echoed flatly. 'In what way?'

'Management offered me a black ops crew of my own choosing—provided I also chose you for your expertise and experience. They spoke of grooming me for the top job. Your name was mentioned. In a partnership. A working one. A personal one. I felt as if they were handing you to me on a plate.'

It took a lot to make Rowan lose her cool, but she was getting there. She sipped at her water and set it carefully on the bar-top while she tried to stem the angry tirade of words that wanted to spew forth.

'If you want to stop working for Section, then stop.' She kept her voice level and her gaze steady. *Good job, Rowan.* 'Believe me when I say that whoring myself out to you—or anyone else—in order to gain power is *not* on my list of things to do. If I want more power I'll damn well go after it on my own, thank you.'

Okay, now she was getting snappy.

'You have vastly underestimated my self-respect.'

'You're sexy when you're riled.' Jared smiled again, his big body relaxing infinitesimally.

She speared him with her meanest glare. 'No. You *don't* get a free pass on this. You *believed* them. You thought I was *in* on it.'

'I never said that.' His mouth hardened. 'I told you

what they said and then I told you what I was thinking. There's a difference.'

'And now you know what *I* think.'

'Exactly.' He lifted his glass and drained it. When his voice came again it was raspy. 'I still want to know you, Ro. It feels good to explore your boundaries.'

A knock sounded on the door, accompanied by a softly spoken 'Room Service…'

He crossed to the door and let in a man and a woman in black and white service uniform. Rowan watched in muddled silence as the two attendants set silver-domed serving trays on the table before crossing to the sideboard and opening it to reveal everything a well-dressed dinner table would ever need. Thirty seconds, tops, and the table had been expertly set for two and a candelabra lit.

'Your main meals will be with you in fifteen minutes,' the older man informed them with a smile, and then left.

'You can leave any time,' Jared offered quietly, but Rowan took a steadying breath, crossed to the table and took a seat instead.

'I'm hungry. I need to eat and relax and I like your company. Will you join me?'

'And make small talk?'

'You could always try telling me about yourself,' she murmured as he took the seat opposite, candlelight and shadows making him even more beautiful.

'When I was eight I wanted to be a submariner,' he said as he reached for the bread. 'When I die I want to be fed to the fishes.'

'Do you think about dying a lot?'

'I think about surviving more.' He broke his bread, put it in his mouth and chewed.

'When I was eight I wanted to be a foreign correspondent news reporter,' she offered.

'Seriously?'

'Yes. I grew up an only child in a very serious household where news ran twenty-four-seven. Foreign correspondents were my rock stars. I guess you had to be there.'

'Chances are I wouldn't have stayed there. I like being outdoors—anything to do with water and swimming in the rain.'

'Is this a song?'

'Feel free to add your own verse,' he offered generously.

'I like scalding hot showers, with multiple shower heads.'

'Hedonist.'

Their conversation continued, sporadic and easy, as they ate their way through plates of truly excellent appetisers.

The fact that Jared *wanted* to be open and honest with Rowan didn't mean that it came effortlessly to him. It had been years since he'd last shared pieces of himself with anyone, even if she *did* make it easy for him.

And then their main meals arrived, and he tried not to let the silence ratchet up his tension again. Every scrape of cutlery on a plate fed his senses. Every taste and touch—every glance—branded straight through his skin to enflame the beast beneath.

When she pushed her plate aside at the end of the meal and leaned back in her chair to study him he was hard-pressed not to start trembling, his need to reach out and take was so big.

'Ro...'

He wished his voice worked better, but all he could manage was a gravel-scrape across the vowel. He needed to lose himself in sensation, sink so deeply into it that there was no thought for anything but pleasure, no thought of anything but sex. No room for memories, no way to screw up.

'How do you like your sex?'

And she looked at him with those all-seeing eyes and just knew where he was going with this.

'Soft and sweet not really going to cut it for you?' she asked.

'No. And I don't want to break anything. You, especially.'

'I'm hungry,' she murmured. 'It's been a while for me. If we do this, I don't mind getting a little reckless.'

She was saying all the right words, and her delivery was malt-whisky-smooth. Then again, she'd read his psych report.

'I'm trying to be honest here.' And maybe—just maybe—he was trying to avert disaster. 'I'm touch-starved, apparently. And I'm hungry for you. I've been sitting here fighting the need to reach for you. And it's *big*, this need, and I'm struggling to control it. If we start this... If you want to... I need to know that you'll be okay if I get a little greedy.'

He needed more from her than a simple touch, more than a simple caress, and he didn't know where this would take them or how it would end.

'I usually lead during sex—I take control. But—'

The thought of bringing two years' worth of abstinence to the table and not being able to control himself…

She stood and crossed to the bar, poured him another whisky and brought it to the table, leaning into him and brushing her breasts against his shoulder as she did so. She threaded her fingers through his hair and he closed his eyes on an indrawn breath, unable to do much more than ride the spark of heat that shot from head to groin.

'There is another way we could do this,' she whispered. 'A way to take all that fear of breaking things right out of the equation. Shall I tie you up, Jared? Would that help?'

One hand was still in his hair and the other was tracing a slow trail around his neck. He swallowed hard and nodded as a tremor ripped straight through him.

'Yes.'

She kissed him then, slow and careful—until he framed her face with his hands and let the hunger lick through him.

'Get up,' she whispered, so he did.

And somehow they made it to the bedroom without breaking anything.

She undressed him and kept his tie in her hand. He knew that silk was strong—he'd trusted his life to it on more than one occasion—but if she thought one necktie was going to hold him she was mistaken.

The knot she used to bind his hands together in front of him was impressive.

'On your back, on the bed, arms above your head,' she said next, and then crossed the room and reached for the thick silk rope that held the curtains back.

That was more like it…

He groaned, his dignity in tatters, because…*yes*.

She tied his hands to the bedhead—the very centre of the bedhead—and she had to straddle him and lean all over him to do it. Or maybe she didn't have to. Either way, he wasn't complaining. He twisted beneath her, seeking skin with his lips—the soft inner skin of her upper thigh—and tasted salt and sweetness, felt the give in her as she momentarily melted against him, the strength in her as she redoubled her efforts to secure his hands.

The scent of her…he breathed it in. Skin—he wanted more of it. She obliged by lifting her dress up over her body to reveal two lacy scraps of underwear and then she leaned forward again, so that the skin across her ribs was within reach of his lips, and sighed her approval when he went there, and then higher, to the underswell of her breasts. Higher still as she pushed the lace of her bra aside and gave him access to her nipple. He took his time with that, played her soft and sweet, until finally he clamped down and sucked hard, deeply satisfied by the dark flare that lit her eyes. Yes, she'd take more of that.

And then she pulled away and leaned over him again, testing the strength of the ties by curling her hands around his wrists and pulling until the cords drew tight. She trailed her hands along his arms and over his shoulders, slid her body down his and went to work on him. Mapping him with her hands and with her lips, every ridge and valley, she explored him until he was little more than a straining, moaning mess.

'Good?' she whispered.

'Yes.'

And then she blanketed him with her body and started kissing him, languid, messy, got-all-the-time-in-the-world kisses, while her body learned the shape of his and how best she'd fit against it. She kissed him until he was iron-hard and straining for release, slick with promise… He hadn't come from just the touch of a body against his since he was a teenager, but tonight he thought he might.

Would.

If she didn't stop.

His kisses grew harder and more biting—a warning, in the same way his bucking up against her, unseating her, was a warning.

'Rowan,' he growled, and strained at the ties that bound him. 'Don't you make me come like this. I won't forgive you.'

'Relax.' She slid off him, taking away the heat and the warmth of skin on skin, her eyes assessing. 'What do you want next?' Her fingers teased him and he bucked again. 'Ask.'

'Want your mouth on me,' he rasped. 'Want my tongue buried inside you.' He wanted his sex dirty, filthy and glorious, and he wanted Rowan as unhinged as he was.

She did it with a whimper—swivelled around and settled over him—and he'd never felt the lack of hands more as she held herself above him, barely letting him lick at her, let alone feast.

'More.'

She gave it, little by little, and he tried to be delicate with her even as his hunger roared, and then she lapped at him, and flicked her tongue over his crown, and that was the end of any restraint he might have conjured.

There. Right there. Flicking and sucking. And there was nothing else in his world but the taste of her as he feasted. Rowan's scent, Rowan's taste, Rowan's whimpers. *Ro…* Her name was a litany inside his head, and when her mouth came off him with a gasp, and she rested her face against the crease of his pelvis and started swearing, he knew she was close to orgasm.

She came on his tongue, and every muscle in his body was strung so tight he could hardly breathe. He needed his own release the same way he needed air, but not yet… He was nowhere near ready to end this yet.

And then she was turning around again, lining him up and taking him in in tiny increments, and that was exactly the way he wanted her—he wanted to feel everything. The burn in his shoulders, the tug of her teeth scraping against the underside of his jaw, his breath leaving his body on a groan as he thrust up into her.

He'd have had her on her back by now if he hadn't been restrained. He'd have been out of control, too hard for her to handle, too far gone to hold back. But this…

This was exquisite.

She sat up, hands to his chest, and with her eyes never leaving his face steadied herself and used what little weight she had to push his body back against the bed. She scraped her nails across his nipple, paused with one of them between the nails of her finger and thumb, and then pinched it hard. The stab of pain hit his brain like an aphrodisiac.

'So full of you,' she whispered. 'You're everywhere. And I'm almost there again.'

He snapped up into her and was rewarded by another bolt of pain, courtesy of her fingertips digging into his ribs.

This time it did nothing but drag him further out of himself and into that place where only sensation existed.

'You still with me?'

He had to concentrate in order to understand her words.

'Yes.'

'You still want this?'

'Don't you stop now. Don't.'

'Do you want to come now? Like this? Tied up and on your back? So you can only take what I'm willing to give? Is this the kind of sex you need tonight?'

Heaven help him, it was.

'Yes.'

The sounds she made as she started to move mirrored his own...pleasure and pain and utterly intoxicating. And then she leaned back a little more, set up a little roll of her hips on each downward stroke, closed her eyes and went to town.

And that was the end of him.

CHAPTER NINE

ROWAN WOKE BEFORE DAWN. Her body knew her routine as well as her brain did. The hard and heavy weight against her side was Jared West, and his eyes opened to slits when she began to extricate herself from him.

At some point not long after his second orgasm she'd untied him. It had come as no surprise at all to her that he'd immediately gathered her to him and slid into her again, his mouth on hers, slow and coaxing, his hands everywhere, reverent and gentle. Still all about skin on skin... He hadn't seemed to be able to get enough, but his gaze had been sated and slumberous as he'd brought her to orgasm this time with nothing more than his fingers and the feel of him. And he had followed moments later, cursing and shuddering and making her feel more cherished and wanted than she'd ever been.

He was quite something.

Rowan pressed a kiss to the curve of his shoulder in a silent thank you and he smiled just a little bit, his eyes drifting closed again.

'Time for me to get gone,' she murmured. She still needed to shower and drop by her place for another set of clothes before she went to work. 'Go back to sleep.'

'I'll take you home,' he mumbled, still all sleep-mussed and relaxed.

'Stay. I'll grab a taxi.'

'I'm taking you wherever you want to go. Don't argue.'

It was hard to argue with a sleep-sweet man. 'Stubborn.'

'I like to call it determined.'

She trailed her fingers over his outstretched arm and watched his body respond as if he'd been made for her touch. Heady stuff, but it wasn't real. The state he was in at the moment he'd respond that way to anyone with half a clue about the kind of release he needed. She shouldn't read anything into it.

'May I shower here?' she asked him.

'You don't need to ask.' His eyes had opened to slits again. 'Did you read anywhere that I'm not a morning person?'

'No, but I'm observant.'

'Coffee, Ro. Coffee's the solution.'

'Or you could go back to sleep?'

She patted his hand and slipped from the bed.

The bathroom was full of the kind of expensive shower gels and moisturisers that Ro adored. The shower rose was as big as a dinner plate and delivered enough pressure to make her groan. She felt well used this morning, a little tender in places as she sluiced up and washed away the remnants of last night's lovemaking.

She looked in the mirror once she'd finished and saw a slight woman with small breasts, slender hips, and a funny face that had always been unique rather than beautiful. She leaned closer and looked into her eyes and felt every single one of her forty years. No make-up, just pale porcelain skin and lines of responsibility etched around her eyes and between her brows.

Too old for him, a nagging voice whispered, and she couldn't silence it.

She was too caught up in her work to have any sort of meaningful relationship. Last night…Jared West… she'd known what he'd needed, that was all, and she'd offered a mutually beneficial exchange, seeing as their wants and needs had coincided.

Why, then, did last night feel like such a precious gift?

He was up and moving when she came out of the bathroom wearing yesterday's clothes and a dusting of make-up. He had his jeans on and his shirt in hand and he smiled and slipped past her on his way to the bathroom.

'Give me five minutes,' he murmured.

She should leave.

Instead she headed for the kitchenette and finished what he'd started when it came to the making of coffee. It wasn't going to be particularly *good* coffee, mind, but the little machine was doing its best and she was grateful for it.

Jared joined her a few minutes later, and the expression of pure appreciation on his face would have been gratifying indeed had it been directed at her rather than at the beverage.

'Thanks,' he muttered when she pushed the mug towards him.

'My pleasure.' She smiled wryly. 'How do you feel this morning?'

He took his time answering. 'Quiet. Empty. I slept. You? How do *you* feel?'

Rowan held steady under the sudden intensity of his gaze. 'Responsible,' she offered truthfully. 'Wary.'

She watched his gaze harden.

'You don't need to be either of those things.'

'Grateful,' she said next, and sipped her coffee and studied him over the rim of the mug. He was pretty when he scowled. 'Grateful for your trust.'

He ran his hand through his hair and for a moment he looked so lost.

'I'm not—' he began. 'I'm not always like that in bed.'

'What are you usually like?'

'Dominant.'

'Sometimes people switch.'

He didn't look convinced. 'Not me. Not often. Ro… last night was all about me, and I'm sorry, because it shouldn't have been. What do *you* want out of this? What do *you* need?'

Now it was Rowan's turn to feel lost and uncertain. 'I don't know what I want from you, or what I'm likely to need. I enjoy your company. Your body.' And, truth be told, she enjoyed his current vulnerability.

His gaze skated to her bare upper arm. 'I know it's a little late, but what about pregnancy?'

'I have long-term contraception in place.' A lot of agents did.

'I figured,' he muttered. 'Still should have checked.'

'It wasn't just your responsibility.'

'Yeah.' He ran his hand through his hair—that nervous gesture of his again. 'Things are different with you in the mix. I'm getting that loud and clear.'

'Is that a bad thing?'

He set his coffee down abruptly, took hers from her suddenly nerveless fingers as well. And then he framed her face and kissed her, and she felt the hunger and the desperation in him all the way to her soul. By the time he pulled back they were both breathing hard and her hunger was probably a match for his.

'No, it's not bad at all,' he muttered roughly. 'You scare the hell out of me. *I* scare the hell out of me. But I want more of this. Whatever this is.' He pulled back. 'I'm going to make some decisions today—career and lifestyle-altering decisions. I hope you'll bear with me. I hope you'll still want me.'

'Jared—' She badly wanted to see his confidence return, along with devilry and laughter. She wanted life for him, and peace. 'I think that's a given.'

Jared sat at his temporary desk in the open-plan cubicle that was meant to be an office and stared at the two identical reports he'd just handwritten. He'd given them everything that he'd held back the first time. Every person who'd come looking for Antonov's wares during his time with the man, every name he knew, the connections he'd fathomed, the business framework the now-deceased arms dealer had built. Handwritten—all of it. Not a copy in existence. No cards left to play any more.

He was finished.

Management had asked him for a decision yesterday and he'd stalled them. Turned out he hadn't needed much more time in order to make his decision after all. He didn't have anything to pack—his desk was empty. He didn't have anything to wipe from the computer in front of him because in the short time he'd been back he'd never used it. Save to open emails and ignore them.

He made his way up to the management office he'd been in yesterday and stopped ten feet in front of the secretary-who-wasn't-a-secretary, waiting for her to acknowledge him.

He didn't have to wait long.

'Jared.' She sounded cautious beneath the overlay of pleasant. She looked as if she knew his answer already and was simply waiting for him to voice it.

'I have a report for you. It discloses the information I gathered during my time with Antonov. I hope it's useful.'

She didn't even look at the sheaf of papers he placed on the table. 'So you're leaving us?'

'Yes. I like the woman you chose for me. I'm flattered that you think I could ever partner with her to run the division. I'd learn a lot from her, I think. And from you.' He nodded towards the door on the left. 'And from him. I respect what you do here and the skills required to do it. But the wellbeing of my family will always come first with me and every last one of my siblings is in a good place at the moment, living good lives that they've created for themselves. I don't want to cut myself off from them and I don't want to lure them into the shadow world you're offering. My resignation is at the end of the report.'

She regarded him solemnly. 'It's true, this life is not for everyone. We appreciate you considering it.' She looked at the report. 'Would you be willing to consult with us on occasion?'

'If it's only my skills you want, yes. If you want access to the resources the rest of my family has access to, then no.'

'I'll make a note. Thank you for the report. Your resignation is effective immediately. Is there anything else?'

'No.' He made to take his leave.

'Mr West? If you're dropping by Section Five on your way out, tell Director Farringdon I'd like to see her when she has a moment.'

'Of course.' He hesitated. 'Has anyone ever sat in the top job by themselves?'

'Of course they have.' She smiled slightly. 'And may again.'

Rowan was on a conference call when he went to see her, according to Sam.

'How long will she be?'

'They're just getting started.'

'I only need a minute.'

'Not possible.' Sam eyed his duffel bag with suspicion. 'Going somewhere?'

'To pick up a yacht and then to my brother's beach house. I'm done here. I resigned this morning. I need one minute with her. I want to drop something on her desk. She doesn't even have to break her call.'

'You're welcome to leave whatever it is with me.'

'I'd rather hand-deliver it. C'mon, Sam. One last indulgence and then you'll never have to indulge me again.'

'Uh-huh?' she said dryly. 'I'll see you in. Don't talk if she's sitting at her desk with headphones on. Fair warning.'

'I won't.'

Sam opened the door to the inner sanctum for him and he walked in and saw her sitting behind the desk, headset in place and her desk covered in papers. The expression on her face was a captivating combination of intense focus and serenity—as if this world was one she enjoyed...as if she'd been shaped for it.

She'd told him she'd been working towards it since she was in her teens.

Jared smiled a little at the eyebrow she raised in his direction. He withdrew the second copy of his report and held it up for her perusal before setting it on her desk, picking up her pen and scribbling on it that there were only two such reports in existence and that Management had the other one.

She read the words, nodded, and kept right on listening. *Later?* she scribbled on a memo pad, and he shook his head.

Beach house for me, he scribbled back, and then, belatedly remembering, *Management wants to see you when you're free.*

She frowned at him then, and spoke into the headset speaker. 'Yes, Clayton. I understand.'

He took one more look at her, just in case it was the last one he ever got of her in her workplace element.

He memorised her face.

And then he left.

It took Jared until Friday to get his new yacht to its new home at the marina near the beach house. Five days of putting the craft through its paces and rediscovering the beauty of Australia's eastern coastline as seen from the Pacific. Five days of the sun on his face and shoulders and the spray of the ocean sandpapering his skin.

There had been two storm fronts and he'd revelled in the challenge of them. He'd slept better for being tossed around and catching snippets of sleep whenever he could...far better than he'd slept in any bed lately— with the exception of the bed he'd slept in with Rowan.

He'd slept after she'd tied him up and slaked her thirst for him and his for her.

He'd slept heart to heart and skin to skin with her name on his lips.

Her name was still echoing in his head and in his heart, deep in his psyche. Altering his perceptions. Changing his way of thinking about things. He'd left a message on her phone, telling her where he was going, what he was doing, and saying that he'd be in touch with her again once he'd docked. He'd invited her to the beach house, if she wasn't doing anything this weekend.

He didn't want to hear her say no. The little bird of hope in his chest just didn't want to hear it. So he hadn't rung again.

When he docked mid-morning on Friday, he didn't interrupt Rowan's work-day by calling. He let the little bird keep right on fluttering and called Lena instead, asked her if she wanted to meet him at the marina and take a look at their new purchase. He knew it for a token question because he knew full well she'd be there within the hour—her curiosity wouldn't have it any other way.

If he was lucky she'd bring lunch.

She came by the swift red speedboat that Jared had forgotten she possessed. It had been a present from Trig, and Jared had got into trouble once for stealing it.

He smiled at the memory as Lena tossed a rope up to him with a cheerful 'Looking good, brother.'

Lena looked beautiful and carefree, sun-browned and happy. She handed him a bright red Esky next, and then put her hand up for him to haul her aboard.

He laughed. 'Wait for the ladder.'

'I don't need a ladder—just give me your hand.'

'With my ribs? Hell, no. You look heavy.'

'I'm a lightweight these days, I shall have you know,' she protested. 'My husband can carry me easily. You're just getting careful in your old age.'

'Had to happen some time. I'm also world-weary and jaded—and as of three days ago unemployed.'

'Good thing you're independently wealthy, then.'

He set the ladder over the side, and only when she'd reached the top did he offer his hand and some of his strength to help her board.

'Nice,' she said, looking around the little craft. 'I thought you said it was second-hand?'

'It is. Although I don't think the previous owners ever actually sailed it anywhere.'

'Good for them.' Lena grinned. 'Better for us.' She headed for the hatch and leaned down to look inside. 'Dear God, it's *mustard*!'

'It's soothing.'

'You're joking.' She started down the hatch. 'Damon's wife, Ruby, has the most amazing eye for colour. I say we let her loose on it.'

'Isn't she a little busy right now? With a baby coming?'

'Okay, you're right, I'll do it myself. Maybe Ruby and the baby can help. You realise that I fully intend to be the mad aunt who leads that child astray every chance I get? He'll have West genes to contend with—shouldn't be too hard.'

'He?'

'Or she. I have no preference. I just want a beautiful healthy baby for them.'

'You're not—? You don't—? I mean…'

He had no idea how to ask his next question, but Lena took pity on him.

'Am I jealous?' She nodded, but her wry smile held no bitterness. 'A little. I'm kind of still coming to terms with the fact that no child will ever carry my blood, but there are other options. Adoption. Surrogacy. Even fostering. I met a twelve-year-old boy in hospital last year when I was there. He's still there. The rest of his immediate family died in the same car accident that damaged his pelvis and legs.'

'You want to take him on?'

'Thinking about it. He's a sweet kid. Never gives up. He'd fit right in.'

'Does he have any other family?'

'A grandmother on his maternal side who loves him dearly. But her resources are limited.'

'Would she give him up?'

'I don't know that I'd even ask that of either of them. I'm thinking more along the lines of encompassing them both.'

'Where does she live?'

'Byron. That's the beauty of it. She wouldn't necessarily have to relocate. If we can show that between us we have all Tom's rehabilitation, schooling, social and emotional needs covered we could bring him home from hospital.' She shoved her sunglasses atop her head and fixed him with a penetrating stare. 'What do you think?'

'I think that if anyone can make it work, you can.'

He'd stood in front of the head of special intelligence only a few days ago and the older man, upon hearing Lena's name, had questioned what she would bring to a team in her current state.

Heart. She would have brought that.

'Management asked me to put together a black ops

team the other day. If I'd have done so you'd have been in it. No—correction. I'd have asked you to be in it.'

Her smile faded.

'I turned the offer down. Didn't want it. Would you have wanted it?'

She looked at him for a long time and then slowly shook her head. 'No. Once upon a time, hell yes. But, no—not any more.'

'Then I guess I did the right thing.'

'I guess you did.'

She studied him intently, as if she couldn't quite get a good read on him, and it shattered him to know how closed-off he'd become these past two years—even to family.

'So how does it feel to be free of it?'

He looked out over the ocean and thought of the days he'd just experienced. The stirrings of a new beginning in them…and a woman he'd never forget.

'Feels good.'

Lena's smile was blinding and her hug was fierce, and then she fell back and let him find his footing when it came to all the pesky emotions running through him.

'Lunch? I need to investigate the mustard colour further. And the fittings. Bring the Esky.'

She disappeared down the hatch completely this time, and all he heard then was her voice—no visual to go with it—but it made him laugh regardless.

'*Seriously?*' Her voice had risen an octave. 'You bought a yacht with purple floral curtains?'

'Told you the owners weren't sailors.'

'Yes, but you've been sailing this poor wee boat for how long? And you haven't yet taken them *down* yet?'

'I've been preoccupied.'

He hadn't actually registered them as offensive—just unnecessary—and with the absence of anywhere to toss them… He started down the steps and found half the curtains and their strings already on the ground.

'You'd better not be touching my half. I like them.'

'You do not.'

The rest of them were down before he even had the food on the bench and his sister stood, hands on her hips, surveying the interior of the yacht—which admittedly seemed much brighter now.

'Much better. I'm even warming to the mustard leather. At least the walls are white.'

Not everywhere. 'Bedrooms are that way,' he said with a tilt of his head—and waited for her reaction.

She looked. 'Oh, for the love of— Someone skinned a spotted cow and draped it all over your bedroom.'

'You mean *your* bedroom. I took the other one.'

'Oh, no. No way. She who paid her half first gets first choice of the bedrooms.'

She opened the door to the other bedroom and Jared didn't have to wait long at all for her screech.

That bedroom had purple and mustard walls with black and white hatbox trim. And a lime-green shag pile carpet. The second bedroom was awesome.

'This isn't a yacht—it's a sideshow palace,' she said, turning to flick him a quick grin. 'I can't believe you bought it.'

'It had been on the market for a while. Do you love it? I love it.'

'We're getting Ruby in. This is beyond me. I know my limits.'

There were a lot of limits in place these days. Many of them learned the hard way.

'She sails well,' he said of the yacht. 'Like an angel.'

'What a *good* girl. Does she sail *now*?'

And that was how they ended up moored off Green Island, swimming from boat to beach, later that afternoon.

Lena lay in the shallows, content to be buffeted by gentle waves. Jared sat next to her and wondered at the inner peace that he'd somehow found between one day and the next. Walking away from his job. Sleeping with a woman he'd connected with on a level that had left him wrung out and craving more.

'What do you think of Rowan Farringdon?'

Lena lifted her head to look at him. 'In what capacity?'

'For me.'

Long black lashes swept down over her sister's eyes. 'Well, she's not dumb.'

'But?'

'Is it even possible for someone in her position to have a decent relationship? A sharing and caring one, with someone who's not involved in that world any more?'

'I don't know.'

'Is that the kind of relationship you even want?'

He shrugged and she splashed him with water—a great swathe of it, driven by her outstretched arm.

'You need to get in touch with your feelings,' his sister told him.

'Says the woman who spent ten years ignoring her own feelings, when it came to who *she* loved.'

'So I'm slow? Not exactly a newsflash.'

'You're not slow.'

It was an old scold that went way back to when schoolwork had come so easily to him and his younger siblings but Lena had had to work hard for every mark she received. She'd despaired of her inadequacies, and sometimes she still did.

'Wash your mouth out.'

She grinned at him, more mermaid in that moment than human soul. 'I missed you,' she murmured. 'I'm glad you're back, and I'm selfish enough to like the fact that you've quit a job that would have swallowed you whole. I like it that you're finally showing more than a passing interest in a woman, even if I'm not entirely sure she's going to be able to give you what you need.'

'What *do* I need?'

'Someone who can be there for you the way you'd be there for them. It's a big ask. Because I know full well the lengths you'll go to for the people you love.'

Jared stared out over the blue sky and the darker blue of the ocean. 'I like her. There's something about her.'

'So keep me posted?'

'That'd be telling.'

'Yes.'

He didn't have to turn to see the smirk on her face.

'Yes, it would.'

CHAPTER TEN

ROWAN TOOK THE weekend off. She'd worked the last three weekends in a row and she was entitled to some down time. She headed for the airport, got on a plane, and three hours later touched down at a little regional airport in northern New South Wales.

And found Jared waiting for her.

Oh, she could get used to this.

He was good at making a woman feel special.

Offer her a crooked smile and a searching glance and the job was done.

'Where are we going?' she asked, and it was good to know that she hadn't had to organise anything about this weekend beyond turning up to it.

'Beach house tonight. Sailing tomorrow. Lena's for late-afternoon drinks when we get back, and then beach house again on Saturday night. How does that work for you?'

"Beautifully.' It sounded a whole lot like heaven.

'Do you have to be anywhere on Sunday?' he asked.

'I did have an invite to Sunday dinner with my parents, but I cancelled on them.'

'Is that going to cause a problem?'

'I get the feeling they were expecting it. My parents

recently retired and they're feeling invisible. They're searching for meaning within their new life, people to fill it, but I can't be there for them the way they want me to be. Except for my grandfather, I don't really do family.'

'Why not?'

'Because there isn't any.'

He fell silent after that, and so did she as they headed towards a four-wheel drive tabletop ute, with fishing rod racks and surfboard racks gracing its roof.

'I'm glad you came,' he said as he stowed her carry-on bag in the back and opened the door for her.

'So am I.'

'I'd kiss you, but I want to get you home first.'

'Is this a control thing?'

He smiled down at her, slow and sweet. 'It's a once-I-start-I-don't-aim-to-stop thing.'

Maybe it came naturally to him, or maybe he'd had a lifetime's practice, but this man knew instinctively how to make her feel like the most precious person in the world.

And Rowan loved him for it.

Jared figured that asking Rowan how her working week had gone was off-limits. He told her what his family was up to, what he'd been up to, and that took five minutes. He made a late supper for them out of mussels and broth and chunky bits of bread and her eyes warmed even as she demolished it.

'Are you on call?' he asked, and she shook her head around a mouthful of food.

No.

'White wine?'

Yes.

He'd been seducing women since his late teens. Confidently. Effortlessly.

This was different.

'Beds and bedrooms are down the hall.' Not exactly the smoothest introduction to their potential sleeping arrangements. 'There's plenty of them.'

'I'm thinking yours.'

Well, all righty, then.

But he didn't rush to get her there. He wanted to take his time.

They headed for the deck after dinner, and maybe Rowan guessed that it was one of his favourite places and maybe she didn't, but in the end they had the big-screen television out there as well, along with enough pillows, cushions and deckchair mats to sleep twenty.

Open-air movie night, and the movie Rowan chose for them to watch was a spy one. They rewrote it as they watched, and Rowan laughed and drank another glass of wine, and pretty soon it was going on for one a.m. and her head was resting on his chest and her eyes were closed and her breathing was regular and deep.

Jared knew what bone-deep tiredness felt like and he had a sneaking suspicion that Rowan was no stranger to it either. He turned off the big screen and the lights and let the stars shine down on them. He dragged pillows towards them, pulled a cover over, tucked her into his side until they fitted together like pieces of a puzzle, and followed her into oblivion.

And the little bird inside his chest—it was singing.

Rowan woke before dawn—it was just her way. She'd been doing it for too many years to adjust easily to waking at a later time.

This time, however, she woke to a sea of pillows and blankets, the sky overhead, and a warm weight at her side was—Jared West. And he was a possessive bastard, even in his sleep, if the hand splayed over her heart was any indication. He hadn't pressed her into anything last night. In fact he'd given her what she'd needed. A place to unwind from the pressures of a hellish week, permission to lie back and breathe.

She might have wanted soul-stealing sexual relations, but he'd given her exactly what she'd needed.

She rolled onto her stomach and moments later he followed, awake and tracing gentle fingers down her spine.

'Did you sleep well?' he murmured.

'Mmm.'

'Want to not sleep any more?'

'Mmm.'

How was that even a question, given that his lips were following his fingers down her spine, soft and dragging and wholly reverent? A breaking dawn and the promise of lovemaking. She arched back against him, helpless in her longing for him.

'Want you to be in me.'

He savoured her—there was no other word for it—and she surrendered to the blinding pleasure and the warmth.

He curled his hands around her thighs once he'd finished exploring every dip of her back. He lifted her to his mouth and for a while she thought he might be a sex god. And then he released her, and then blanketed her again as he slid into her, slow and easy, and then she could have sworn he was a sex god.

He rode her slowly, teased and tormented, built a

stairway to the sky for her. She climbed every step of it. And in the light of a new day they climaxed together.

This wasn't sex as she knew it.

This was different.

'Children,' Rowan said to Jared later that afternoon, over a meal of barbecued ocean perch and mixed salad, served on plastic plates on the deck of Jared's yacht. 'What's your view on them?'

'I like them,' he told her. 'Got nothing against them. Not sure I want any.'

'You're young yet. This is only to be expected. Do you envision them anywhere in your future?

'What if I get it wrong?' He gestured with his fork, barefoot and expansive, looking ever more carefree. 'If I fall down on the parenting job the child wears it. Parenthood requires careful consideration.'

Indeed it did.

'What about you?' he asked. 'Do *you* want children?'

'My parents are really bad role models. My grandfather, by his own admission, was neglectful of my mother, and my mother continued the tradition. I figure that if I remain childless the cycle will stop.'

'And I figure that for bull. Do you *want* children? If you had a loving family to raise them in…a village full of caring people to help you…would you want them then?'

Her hesitation told him many things.

'I'd still have to make a lot of lifestyle changes,' she murmured. 'And I'm getting a little old for child-bearing.'

A valid point—but not insurmountable, by his reckoning.

'And I've never really met a man I've felt a compelling urge to have children *with*,' she added quietly. 'I don't know what kind of parent I'd make. What about my job? You know the hours I keep. It took me five days and two IOUs to get this weekend off.'

Jared frowned.

'I gave up on the idea of motherhood when I got the directorship,' she told him. 'I know you don't think that the age gap between us matters, but maybe my ambivalence when it comes to having children *will* matter to you.'

'You're pushing me away?'

'No.' She looked troubled for the first time that weekend. 'I'm letting you in. Telling you about the hopes and dreams I still harbour, as well as the ones I've let go of.'

Jared digested that, as she'd meant him to all along, and then he looked out over the ocean and realised that fatherhood held no appeal for him if the woman by his side didn't want to be a mother. It was one of the more easy decisions he'd made in quite some time.

'How do you feel about being an aunt?'

'I would make a really good aunt,' she told him solemnly. 'Alas, I have no siblings.'

'I have three. And one very pregnant sister-in-law. I figure that if I get in good with her she might let me borrow the kid from time to time. You could tag along.'

Her eyes warmed. 'You're kind of perfect. Don't let anyone ever tell you any different.'

They made it to Lena's for drinks that afternoon, but only just.

And it wasn't because of sailing boats and contrary winds.

Rowan left late Sunday night, and Jared let her be for three days while he tinkered with the yacht.

He wasn't the only one feeling the tyranny of distance when it came to relationships. Trig was back at work in Canberra—a mere twelve-hour drive from the farmhouse—and although his sister was fiercely independent, there was no denying that Lena was missing her husband.

'We could go visit them,' she said on Wednesday afternoon over the phone. 'Do you still have your private pilot's licence?'

'I haven't flown for two years. I'll need a review.'

'Good thing I kept mine up to date, then.'

'Brat. Do we still have a plane?'

'We do.'

'Does it go?' Keeping the Cessna flight-ready had once been *his* task—back before Antonov.

'Of course it goes. What good are toys if you can't use them?' Lena paused. 'So what do you think? Want to go to Canberra? Because I think midweek visits to people we care about are important.'

'I think you're right.'

Rowan liked Thursdays—and never more so than when a blue-eyed devil rang her at six-thirty, while she was still at work, and asked her to dinner that night.

'Why aren't you at the beach house?' she wanted to know.

'Lena decided to implement a must-see-Trig-midweek-and-have-dinner-with-him policy. She also has a plane, so we flew down.'

'You people…'

'You're not going to talk carbon footprints, are you?'

'No, I was going to stick with a comment about obscene wealth instead, but I've changed my mind. It's good to hear from you.'

'And dinner this evening? I know it's short notice.'

It was. Rowan eyed the number of case updates still open on her taskbar, all of which needed to be read and signed off on. Tonight.

'What if I bring dinner to you?' he said into her silence. 'How late do you have to work?'

'Can you give me another hour and a half? After which time I will be well and truly ready to leave.'

'You want me to pick you up?'

'Or you could meet me at my place with food in hand. There would be huge brownie points earned. Enormous. There could be vanilla bean and shaved chocolate ice cream for dessert.'

'Do I need to bring the ice cream as well?'

'No, there's some in the freezer.'

'I'll meet you there,' he said. And hung up.

There was a lot to be said for walking towards the glass-walled lobby of her apartment block and finding a beautiful man waiting for her with a bag full of takeaway food dangling from his fingers.

She watched those fingers tighten as she walked towards him, watched him catalogue everything about her—from the shoes she wore to the colour of her lipstick.

She wondered if he saw what she saw. A woman of average height and mediocre looks. A woman who—on a personal level—people rarely waited around for.

The closer she got the better he looked. The smell of delicious food wafted towards her, mixing and mingling with the faintest scent of *him* as she leaned in to brush her lips against his face, first one cheek and then the other.

His gaze lingered on her lips for a satisfyingly long time after she drew back, the thrumming stillness of his body a sign that he'd liked her greeting a lot.

He liked her lips—she remembered that.

Gave thanks for that.

They got in the elevator and she pressed the button for the top floor. He didn't crowd her. He just watched.

'Come on in,' she murmured when finally she opened the door to her apartment, more than a little curious as to what he would make of her home.

Neutral colours for the walls and a pale wooden floor, richer caramels and ivory colours for the bigger furniture items. No knick-knacks…a couple of family photos. She liked colour, and had added it in the form of cushions and throw rugs, the textures soft and inviting. The views from the windows were of the surrounding cityscape and nothing special. None of it was special.

This place hadn't been designed with looking outward in mind. This place was for curling up in, intimate and engulfing. The hotel apartment he'd taken her to had been bigger and better outfitted.

'It isn't much. One bedroom, a couple of bathrooms, one study and this space. I've never—'

He followed her through to the kitchen and set the food on the counter. 'Never what?'

She was for ever revealing her innermost thoughts to him. 'I don't entertain here much.'

'It's your cave,' he murmured. 'I get it. And I'm flattered that I got an invitation. No pressure, okay? You want me to leave—just show me the door.'

'I don't want you to leave.' And it wasn't just because

the food containers he'd started lining up on the kitchenette bench held so much promise. 'Is that pork belly with plum sauce on the side, green beans and mashed potatoes from my second favourite restaurant?'

She might have been guilty of telling him about the dish on the weekend and waxing lyrical.

'It is. When did you last eat?'

Rowan rubbed at the frown between her eyes. 'Maybe around eleven?'

'And you started when? Six?'

She nodded, and he speared her with a penetrating glance.

'Work. Sleep. Eat. Play. *Balance*, Ro. Haven't you ever heard of it?'

'Says the man who up until a couple of weeks ago lived his work twenty-four-seven. Undercover.'

'And I have learned my lesson.'

She dumped a handful of serving spoons on the counter and he picked one up and started dishing food out.

'More potato?'

'Yes. Always yes to that question. How long are you here for?'

'We'll leave again tomorrow night and take Trig with us for the weekend. You too, if you want?'

Rowan hesitated. Much as she wanted to, her dance card was already full. 'Sorry. I'm on call. And I have a date with an octogenarian.'

'Your grandfather?'

'You should meet him. I think you'd like him.'

Jared stilled, and then carefully, casually, continued serving.

'I saw that hesitation,' she murmured. 'Too soon to talk of having you meet my favourite person?'

'No, I— It wasn't that.' It was as close to a mumble as he ever got. 'You said I should meet him and I instantly thought yes. Which gave me pause—because normally there *is* a pause while I try to figure out how to say no thanks.'

'You probably only want to meet him because he's a retired general who owns a pet tortoise called Veronica.'

'Veronica, huh?'

'You should probably compliment the General on her superbly patterned shell. He's very proud of her.'

'I have absolutely no idea whether you're setting me up or not.' His smile warmed her. 'But I like it. Where are we eating? Bench or table?'

'Table.'

He really was deliciously easy to accommodate. They sat and ate, and Rowan tried not to bolt her food, but it was so good, and— *Oh*.

'What would you like to drink?' So much for her skills as a hostess.

'Relax. I'll get it.'

He came back with soda water for both of them and she looked at the drinks and grimaced in embarrassment. Soda water, still water or milk had been his only choices.

'I really wasn't expecting you tonight. If I had I would have magically arranged for my fridge to be fuller.'

He smiled, slow and contented. 'I really don't care if your fridge is full or not.'

So there was that, and his apparent ease with her living arrangements, and a slow-building heat that made her wonder whether it would be appropriate to push her meal aside, crawl across the table and feast on *him*.

Instead, she chose small talk. 'What have you been up to?'

'Racing speedboats and thinking about my future. Last time I decided on a career path I didn't think of anything beyond superficialities.'

'All the pretty toys?' she murmured.

'Exactly.' He speared a pork square and offered it to her—and who was she to refuse? 'These days I'm older, wiser and more searching. I want to feel useful. Money isn't a necessity. I thrive on adrenalin and I'm narrowing down options.'

'What kind of options?'

'Banking. The family business. It'd make my father happy and the stock exchange pit might suit me.'

She studied him in silence.

'No comment?'

'Maybe as a short-term career option, sure...'

His smile turned wry. 'You think I'd get bored?'

'You said it yourself. You're not money-focused. You need a cause.'

'I had a cause once. It was corrupt.'

'Not all of it.'

'Enough to give me pause. I don't want to go to work each day and have to decide who's going to betray me today and who's not. I don't know how you do it. The politics and the conniving. The lack of loyalty.'

'It's not that bad. The politics and the conniving— I'm good at it. As for the loyalty... Well...' Maybe she was simply used to rolling with betrayal. 'I know what you could do,' she began. 'What about something along the lines of what your brother does? Cyber information acquisition? Ask him who's hiring.'

Jared eyed her with a frown. 'Not my thrill.'

'What about physical retrieval?'

'Of what?'

'Anything. Do your homework when it comes to who wants what and why. Pick and choose your jobs carefully. You call the shots.'

He stared at her for a good long while. 'Maybe.'

'It'd suit your lifestyle.'

'And what lifestyle is that?'

'Plenty of action, plenty of travel. No time to get bored because every job would be different.'

'And if I wanted to forgo the travel and stick a little closer to home?'

'Is that what you want?'

He'd surprised her. *Again.* But then, when had he ever not?

'Yeah. My gut says it's time to settle down. Choose a place and make it home.'

'And what does your gut say about you flying in to have takeaway dinner with a woman who can't even keep a meal in her house?'

'My gut says the food's good and yours is the company I want.' His voice had gone all raspy. 'I wanted to see you, Ro. Touch base. Something like that.'

She was still waiting for the other shoe to drop.

'Touch base or just touch? Are you having trouble sleeping again?' Maybe that was why he was here. Maybe he needed the kind of release she'd given him at the apartment.

'I'm sleeping well enough.' His voice had husked out. 'I don't need you to tie me up.'

'Really not a problem if you did.' She put it out there. 'I enjoyed it.'

Hell, she'd *loved* it.

He shrugged again—only this time it was an invitation if ever she'd seen one.

'Not this time.' His eyes had gone dark. 'Stop trying to give me what you think I came here for, Ro. Stop trying to fix me as if I'm broken. Nor is it your job to direct me towards a solution. Otherwise I'm going to start thinking you're still at work.'

'*How* am I directing you?' she asked indignantly. 'I've done no directing at all tonight!'

'No? Then why is the focus all on me and my problems? On what I might need and how I might arrange my life? I didn't bring those topics up, Ro. You did. You're still looking at me as if I'm one of your problems to be solved.'

'No.' Was he right? *Was* she still in work mode? 'I—Maybe I—'

'Yes?' he enquired silkily.

Well, hell. Rowan sat back in her chair and stared at him. Had she still been in work mode? Half of her trying to figure out what he needed so that she could provide support? The other half assuming that he couldn't possibly be there simply because he'd wanted her company. Just her company—nothing more.

'I'm interested in you and I make no apology for some of my questions,' she offered finally. 'How else will I know what's going on in your life if I don't ask? But maybe I do need to ease out of work mode a little more—stop trying to offer up solutions and just…relax now that I'm home. It'll happen. The relaxation part. Any minute now. I'm almost sure of it.'

'Uh-huh?' He loaded up his fork with potato. 'Eat your dinner, Rowan. And then we'll set about seeing what it takes to get you to unwind.'

Rowan filled her mouth with food—it seemed like the best course of action—and at some point during the meal Jared's leg kicked into hers and stayed there.

Not unwinding.

He told her about Lena and Ruby ganging up on him and insisting that mustard was not an appropriate colour for the interior of a yacht. He made her laugh, but he looked at her with an intensity that made it impossible to relax. How was a person supposed to relax into *that*?

'Would you like ice cream now?' she asked when they'd cleared their plates. 'I'll just get—'

'No, you won't. Stay.' He eyed her sternly and took the plates to the dishwasher. 'Do you even *want* ice cream after that? Or is it just something else to offer your guest?'

'I sometimes have ice cream after dinner.'

'Do you want some tonight?'

She was tempted to prove him wrong and say yes—but she'd be lying. She didn't have to stay sitting at the table like a lump, though. It was *her* kitchen. The least she could do was help tidy it.

But he blocked her way and there was pure challenge in his eyes when he murmured, 'It's done, Rowan, and it really doesn't need any final check-up.'

'You think I'm a control freak?'

'I think we're about to find out. Would you like me to tell you what kind of sex I'd like tonight?'

'Um…' Could be a test. 'Your call.'

'Good answer.' He was advancing on her, backing her against the wall, boxing her in with his arms either side of her and his body heat licking at her senses. 'If you want me to leave, tell me now.'

The best answer to that was silence.

'I want to make you forget your own name tonight,' he murmured. 'You good with that?'

'Well, you can try. Are you waiting for permission?'

Her tone would probably have been a lot more challenging had he not been dragging his lips over her neck at the time. Because all she could manage as his tongue got in on the act was a whimper.

By the time he got around to kissing her lips she had her eyes closed and her hands palms to the wall for fear of burying them in his hair and directing him where she wanted him to go. And then he coaxed her shirt up over her head, and when her arms fell they fell to his shoulders.

He didn't need any direction when it came to getting his shirt off, or her trousers either. No direction at all as he picked her up as if she weighed next to nothing, his hands on her buttocks, his strong fingers curling under and around to tease at the edges of her panties.

She was so wet for him. The minute he touched her he would know, if he didn't already, that all he had to do was put his hands on her and she was halfway to gone.

And then his fingers skated across the slick she was making for him, and he growled and slammed her back into the wall, coaxing her legs to open around him— and, *oh*, that worked for her. She spread her legs wider, rocking up into that teasing hardness, letting him know in no uncertain terms that she would like more of that.

'Please…' she whispered into his mouth as she wound her arms around his neck and held on.

Denim rasped against her as she ground up onto him—hard.

'Please. I won't break. Anything you want.'

She wanted to feel his thickness inside her so that she

didn't have to clench around nothing. She wanted the burn that came of trying to swallow him whole.

And then he took her to the counter, hooked his fingers through her panties and pulled them off. He unzipped himself next and pushed his boxers down. He took himself in hand, his eyes almost black as he breached her—just a little. Nothing more than a promise that soon…soon he would fill her up.

He opened her mouth with his thumb next. She sucked it in and got it good and wet before pulling back to nip at the knuckle. *There. All done. Good job.*

He was still toying with her, not giving her nearly enough of his length, and he toyed with her some more as he put his thumb to her centre and rubbed, finding exactly the right spot.

She bit her lip to stop herself from keening, but some sound escaped and his gaze, which had been fixed elsewhere, met hers.

'There? Is that good?'

He knew it was.

His next kiss was filthy—all grazing teeth and demanding tongue.

She was riding the ragged edge of desperation, and he knew she wanted more, but he made her wait even as he built her slowly, inexorably towards climax.

She slapped one hand behind her on the counter for leverage, the better to lift her hips up and forward. Greedy…so greedy…for more pressure from his thumb and an inch or seven more. It wasn't as if he didn't have them to give.

He slid into her a little more—huge, hard and so welcome she could hardly stand it. Almost there…almost.

'What do you want?'

His rumbled words licked at her as she bucked forward and she gained another inch of him, and then cried out her frustration when he wouldn't let her have any more.

But she wasn't going to direct him this time. She didn't always have to call the shots. Sometimes she wanted more than anything to ditch that responsibility and have someone call them for her.

'Anything,' she whispered. 'Whatever you want.'

'Good.' He sheathed himself all the way inside her with one mercifully hard thrust. 'Come.'

CHAPTER ELEVEN

ROWAN WOKE TO a warm and touch-happy man in her bed and didn't mind his presence at all. Not the circle of his arms or his sleepy good morning. Not the way he kept one hand on her stomach even as he rolled over to check his phone.

'What time do you have to be at work?' he mumbled.

She muttered something about six o'clock and pulled his phone towards her so that she could see the time more clearly. She groaned—six o'clock being forty minutes away and all.

'I've got to get up. What time are you and the gang heading back today? Because you're welcome to stay here this morning. Just lock up on your way out.'

'You know what I remember best about my mother?' he said as he pulled her to him and placed a kiss on her temple. 'Whenever my father had to leave for work, be it for a day or for a fortnight, she always got up and saw him off, and he always left smiling. Even back then I liked her priorities.'

Rowan remembered back to those days in far-flung countries when her parents hadn't even bothered to tell her where they were going. She'd simply wake to an amah or the housekeeper telling her they were gone.

Could be why Rowan liked her job so much nowadays. Knowing where people were and what they were doing just flat-out *worked* for her on a psychological level. That kind of information was important to her. It made her feel secure.

'Was she a stay-at-home mum, your mum?'

'Depends on your definition. Companies used to come to her with their figures for analysis. She was a mathematician—an incredibly bright one. I think that's where we all got our smarts from.'

'She sounds like a remarkable woman.'

'Life is full of them.' He turned his head, his eyes as penetrating as any laser. 'You're one.'

'Trust me—I am not that smart.'

'You're a driven, focused, impressively networked problem-solver. And you know I'm more than halfway gone on you. And now we need to get out of this bed before I derail all your good intentions when it comes to you being on time for work.'

Rowan slid out of bed with a light in her heart. She shared her toiletries and her shower with him and smirked her satisfaction when he emerged, hair still spiky and wet, smelling faintly of ginger and roses. She ground beans and made coffee with the sinfully expensive machine that had been a fortieth birthday present to herself, and watched his eyes glaze over when he lifted the steaming black brew to his lips.

This man practically turned into a biddable little lamb in exchange for a morning cup of coffee.

Something to remember.

By the time he was on his second cup she was almost ready to walk out through the door. 'You'll lock up behind you?'

He nodded and set the cup down. 'So… Me coming here to see you during the week. You coming up to the beach house when you can. Is that going to work for you? Because if it does…if you want to try to build some kind of ongoing relationship with me…I'm all for it.'

'An exclusive relationship?'

'I don't share.' His eyes flashed hot with temper. 'We do this and you're mine and no one else's. And I'm yours.'

'Yes.'

She wanted to crawl into his lap and stay there for a week. Gorge herself stupid on him and let him feast on her. She wanted this man and all that he was offering. There would be spats with him, because he wasn't a malleable soul and neither was she. There was a good chance that she would want more than he could give.

But she contented herself with kissing him slow and sweet and savouring this moment of pure happiness. 'Yes,' she whispered. 'Yes, I think that would work.'

CHAPTER TWELVE

On Wednesday the following week Jared got a phone call from Damon. He and Damon didn't really *do* social calls, so his brother's quiet 'Hey, how you tracking?' caught his attention, regardless of the innocuous words.

'Yeah, good. Better than I was.'

'And your ribs? They're good now too?'

Okay, now his brother was getting weird.

Jared strode past the pool on his way to the big double doors that led out onto the deck overlooking the ocean. 'Yeah, they're fine. What's going on?'

'You at the beach house?'

'Yeah. Why? You need it for something?'

'Need you to get something out of the safe for me. I'll call you back in five minutes.'

'Better make it ten. I know that safe, but damned if I can remember the password.'

'You break it—you buy it. Search your memory, brother. I know you have one.'

'You always have to do things the hard way,' Jared grumbled.

'Good to hear you bitching again. I've missed it.'

Damon rang off.

Jared sighed, put the phone back in its cradle and

padded down the long hallway to Damon's study. He'd barely set foot in it since he'd been here. Mostly he used the kitchen, the pool and the beach that beckoned so brightly. He was taking it easy. Feeling his way in this new life and trying not to demand too much from the woman he wanted to be with.

Jared remembered the combination to the safe the moment he looked at it. His brain was good for stuff like that. He scooped up the phone, the computer and the power cords sitting in the safe and took them out to the kitchen and plugged them in. There was nothing else in the safe. This was it.

He made himself a rare roast beef sandwich—tomato, lettuce and pickle included—in the two minutes he had left before Damon rang again. His brother was excruciatingly punctual. If Damon said he'd call back in five minutes, he meant five minutes.

He was mid-bite of his sandwich when one of the 'safe' phones rang. Damon and his insistence on black market phones that couldn't be traced... Mind you, they were useful.

'You know that phone you left in Seb's toiletries bag at the wedding?' Damon began when Jared picked up, referring to their sister Poppy's partner.

'I thought that was *your* toiletries bag?'

'Nope. It was Seb's. Luckily he's a sharing, caring kind of guy and he told me about it. I brought it home with me and I've been keeping it charged. I figured if you wanted it you'd ask for it.'

'Thanks.' Jared eyed his sandwich longingly before putting it down. 'It has information on it that I didn't feel like sharing.'

'Someone called the phone last night.'

'Say *what*?'

'You sound surprised.'

'Only one person ever used that number. And he's dead.'

'It's Antonov's kid, from what I can gather. I'm going to play the messages for you now. First one's just a hang-up call—didn't leave a message,' Damon said. 'The second one's more interesting.'

Damon did something to the phone at his end and Antonov's seven-year-old son's voice came on the line.

'JB? Jimmy? You said to call you if I ever got in trouble, so I'm calling,' the boy said in his native Russian. 'My mother doesn't want me. She thought I'd come with money but there isn't any. And my father's friends don't believe her, and she's scared because they're saying that my father owed them and now she owes them and they're really bad men. She says I'm too sick and that I'm more trouble than I'm worth and that she can't protect me. She doesn't want me.' The boy's voice broke. 'She never did.'

Jared slumped against the counter and closed his eyes against the wash of remorse that slid through him like poison. Antonov's little boy had always been his weak spot when it had come to bringing Antonov's operations to a halt. *What would happen to the sick little boy with Antonov in prison and a mother who'd been nowhere in the picture and didn't want to be?* Only Antonov had died, which had changed the equation again. Celik's mother had become the boy's next of kin and Celik had been shipped off to her.

'You still there?' asked Damon.

'Yeah,' he rasped in a voice that wasn't his. 'I'm listening.'

'This next one came in a couple of hours after the second message.'

Jared waited to hear what the boy had had to say this time.

'You promised I'd be okay. I'm not okay. *Please*,' Celik begged. 'You promised my father that if anything bad ever happened to him you'd look after me. I *heard* you. Can you come and get me?'

The message ended and once again no one spoke.

And then Damon cleared his throat. 'Did you really promise that?'

'Yeah.' His brother hadn't *been* there. 'Yes, I did.'

'I love you, man, and I know you move mountains— you've been my hero ever since I was a kid, think Superman—but how the *hell* do you intend to make good on that promise?'

'I *can* make good on it.' Jared's hands might be trembling but he had to believe it. 'Can you trace the calls?'

'The calls track back to a canal house in Amsterdam, and all three of them came in overnight—my time. Truth be told, I didn't check that phone for messages when I first got up. I didn't even look at the phone until after lunch. It's been silent. I've only being paying cursory attention to it.'

'I never asked you to check for messages. I didn't think there'd *be* any.'

'So what's your plan?'

'Go and get him.' Nothing else he could do.

'You need any help with that?'

He was going to need a great *deal* of help with that. Not to mention some kind of real plan. 'Don't you have a pregnant wife to be with?'

'Just saying that I'm right here if you need anything

by way of information or assistance. I don't have to be there in order to help you. Have computer will cyber-travel, man. If you're planning a covert extraction…if you're aiming to disappear the boy out from under every-one's noses…don't count me out. Count me in.'

'I— Thanks.'

He'd always left Damon out of the loop when it came to the work he'd performed. He'd always left Damon out of the loop, *period*. If Jared were to hazard a guess he'd say that he'd always thought of Damon as too young and unpredictable to take part in any wild scheme he and Lena had dreamed up as teenagers. But his brother wasn't that kid any more.

Courtesy of that damned psych report, Jared now had more than a passing acquaintance with the slights he'd bestowed on his younger brother over the years and the underlying reasons for them.

Damon alive. Their mother dead.

Resentment.

'Yeah. I could probably use your help if you want in,' he muttered gruffly. 'Celik Antonov is a sweet kid. A *good* kid. He doesn't deserve this.'

'Do you have a plan for once you have him?'

'Antonov has a sister. He set her up with an alias and enough money for a simple life twenty years ago and then he left her to it. No contact whatsoever until three months ago, when a Romanian woman contacted him about donating a kidney to his son. A kidney with a high chance of being a match for the kid. Her name was So-phia and Antonov had her on speaker phone. He cut her off. And then he broke down and wept.'

And then the story had come out.

'Did she give the kid the kidney?'

'She never called again.'

'What makes you think she'll take the boy?'

'She offered him her kidney.'

'Do you know where to find her?'

'No, but I know she's a schoolteacher in a small village in Romania and that she's childless. Also that she was worked over by thugs when she was twelve and Antonov was eighteen. Antonov had got on the wrong side of some dangerous people and that was their warning to him. Care to do a bit of sleuthing?'

'Sophia…schoolteacher…Romania…childless and her age,' Damon replied dryly. 'Good thing I'm brilliant.'

'Ah, modesty. Guess it runs in the family. Call me when you have something.'

'You taking anyone with you when you go to get him?'

'Wasn't planning on it.'

'Will you tell Trig where you're going? Or Lena? *Anyone?*'

'Are you insinuating that I need to share more with the family?'

'*Yes*. Save yourself a repeat of Lena going after you. Again. Because she will—and she'll drag us all into it.'

'Consider them told.'

Somewhere in the past two years Jared had lost control of his family entirely. Something to rectify. Eventually…

'Hey, Damon?' Jared considered his next question carefully. 'I'm going to need a handler on this job. I need someone to plan ahead with. Someone to talk me through the options once I'm on the ground and steer me in the direction that's safest for the kid… Would you do it?'

'Are you asking me?'

There was something in Damon's voice that sounded a whole lot like hope. Willingness—that was in there too. Need, even.

'Yeah, I'm asking you. And I know exactly what kind of responsibility it entails, so if you don't want—'

'I'll do it,' his brother said gruffly. 'Who better, right? It's not as if I'd want anyone else doing it.'

'Okay.' Jared cleared his throat. 'Okay, thanks.'

This family.

There was silence then, while their relationship settled into new territory, and then Jared took a deep breath. 'This Amsterdam canal house? Where do I find it?'

'I'll send you directions. You going to ring the kid?'

'You going to give me the number?'

The answer to both was yes.

Rowan hated it when someone else's plan went awry and landed on *her* desk. She'd been keeping tabs on Antonov's son from a distance, touching base with the officials responsible for placing the boy with his mother. So far she didn't think much of their decisions. 'Set and forget' being their preference.

The child's mother was a high-class courtesan who'd held Antonov's attention long enough to beget him a child. He'd paid her handsomely for her trouble and she'd given up the child without a backward glance.

That was then.

These days Celik's mother worked even more selectively, operating out of her own home in the middle of Amsterdam. She wasn't a criminal, and she enjoyed a comfortable standard of living. She didn't take drugs and didn't drink to excess. On paper, sending Celik Antonov to live with his birth mother once his father was dead had seemed like an obvious solution.

Until one started factoring in the late arms dealer's enemies and alliances.

The boy's mother was smart, but she was currently beset by vultures she didn't have the resources to deal with. She was out of her league.

It was time to do something.

Rowan sighed and reached for the phone.

She waited until the man that she and all the other directors answered to picked up. She needed to cover all bases with this one—her own base included.

'Sir, I have the latest report on Celik Antonov in front of me. I'd like permission to bring Jared West back in on the case in an advisory capacity. He knows the child and he understands the situation. I'd like to run certain scenarios on relocation for the child past him.'

Her request was reasonable. She was just doing her job. But there was more to her request than that.

'I also think Jared would want to be notified of this. It was his case. His fallout.'

And Jared would see it as his problem to fix.

There was silence on the other end, and then that dry, deep voice spoke. 'Jared, eh?'

'Yes, sir.' She'd known that the use of Jared's first name wouldn't go unnoticed. She wanted full disclosure on this. 'I'm intimate with him. This is the one case within my portfolio that I would share with him—with your permission.'

Rowan's palms were sweaty. Not only was a child's wellbeing at stake, so too was her fledgling romantic relationship. It wouldn't sit well with Jared that she had fresh information on Celik that she hadn't passed on to him. She *needed* a yes from Management on this.

'Sir…?'

Could be there had been a whole lot of pleading in that one little prompt. Could be she'd just altered the course of her own career irrevocably.

'Do it,' he said, and hung up.

Rowan slumped back in her chair and ran a clammy palm down over her face in relief.

One down. One to go.

Rowan put a call through to Jared next, knowing full well that he wasn't going to like hearing that the child's situation needed a rethink.

But all she got was an answering machine.

CHAPTER THIRTEEN

JARED ARRIVED IN Amsterdam and made the city his own. Bicycle- and pedestrian-friendly, creatively organised and full of water, the city appealed to him. The water-craft weren't like the ones he'd grown up with, and the canals were a rats' maze, but the place was beautiful and free-wheeling and it appealed to him on a visceral level.

He'd have liked to see Celik grow up here in safety, but that wouldn't happen so long as Antonov's parasites kept after him. Celik's perceived inheritance was the magnet, but the authorities had frozen it. No one could get to it. Not Celik's mother—bless her non-maternal soul—not Antonov's debtors, nor his creditors. That money wasn't going anywhere.

Two years ago he wouldn't have hesitated to go in and take the child, with no one any the wiser. These days his world was not nearly so black and white.

Undercover work had shown him the many facets of every situation. Likewise, Rowan's approach to problem-solving took into account and tried to balance many different needs. Celik had a mother—a woman who had taken him in—and before Jared put any plan for the boy in motion he needed to talk to her and take her needs into consideration.

Jared *wasn't* going into this guns blazing.

He thought Rowan would approve.

Getting to see Celik's mother was easy.

Damon invented an obscenely wealthy, fully verified background for him and booked him an appointment. Two hours, four-thirty to six-thirty p.m., cash only.

Damon's wicked sense of humour at work, but it gave him a cover persona and a trail leading nowhere should anyone decide to investigate.

Damon had invented another persona for Jared as well. In this one he was a highly skilled government operative, specialising in witness protection. It was this second persona that Jared had to sell to Celik's mother in order for any of their plans to work.

He was here to lie, scheme, to light a fire and destroy a little property, and kidnap a child and possibly the child's mother as well.

Every one of those activities should have given him pause.

And they didn't.

Needs must.

He had a plan, finessed by Damon, and he was running with it.

At four-thirty p.m. exactly Jared entered a narrow street paved with cobblestones and walked towards house number twenty-three. The entrance door was flanked by flowerpots filled with colourful blooms. An ornate wrought-iron railing guided visitors up the three steps to the deep red door with its brass lion knocker. The house itself stood three storeys tall—one of Amsterdam's historic 'Gentleman's Houses', abutting one of Amsterdam's oldest canals. Prime real estate, carefully tended and exclusive.

He rang the bell, and was surprised when Celik's mother opened the door herself.

He knew what she looked like from the photos Damon had sent him. He'd been expecting polish and he got it. She was a very beautiful woman in her late twenties, with a face that had an innocence to it that couldn't possibly be real, given her profession. But she had a kind of vulnerability—and her smile was sweet as she asked him his name and then stood back to let him in, waiting until the door had closed behind him.

She led him into a small sitting room filled with deep armchairs and elegant furnishings before asking him for more formal identification.

'A driver's licence, if you please, or a passport.'

He handed her the passport Damon had secured for him and she took a photo of it with her phone and presumably sent it somewhere, presumably for safekeeping.

Not a foolish woman, by any means.

'Precautions,' she said, with another sweet smile. 'Should you become a regular patron, this part of the afternoon can, of course, be dispensed with. My name is whatever you want it to be this evening. Would you care for a drink?'

'I'm really not here for what you think I'm here for.'

He pulled out the second set of credentials and handed them over and watched her innocent expression fade, to be replaced by sharp-eyed consideration.

'I'm here in collaboration with Dutch and Russian officials. I work for an organisation that relocates certain individuals—if that's what they need. I'm here to offer you and your son entry into a witness protection programme.'

Would she do it? He had a plan in place, just in case she said yes.

But neither he nor Damon had judged it likely.

'No.' He watched in silence as her pretty face contorted into a mask of pain and frustration. 'Yes, I requested help, but this is *not* what I want!'

He and Damon had judged correctly.

'Witness *protection*?' she continued angrily. 'Why should I give up my life here when this was never the arrangement? I bore that man a child, yes. A sick child that I couldn't care for. The child's father paid me to go away and stay away—and I *did*. That child upstairs was three days old when I walked away from him. I have the paperwork to prove it. I made no claim on him, or on any fortune he might some day inherit. I have paperwork for that as well. But does anyone care? No! "You're his mother," they said. "He's your problem now—*you* deal with it."'

Not a lot of maternal instinct in that heart.

'Look, he's a sweet kid. He's soft. He has this *innocence*...' she continued. 'How *that* happened, given that father of his, I have no idea. But I can't protect the boy from who he is and what his late father owes. I don't have access to the money his father's business associates want. I don't have the weapons they want. I was never in Antonov's confidence. But these people...they don't want to hear that.'

'You fear for your safety?'

'Yes!'

'I'm offering you and your son a chance to leave this place and start afresh. Somewhere Antonov's debtors won't find you.'

'Take the boy—yes. If he goes away my problems

will disappear. Take him. Please. And leave me out of it. I have a life here—and it's a good one.'

'If that's what you want…' He'd been counting on it. 'I require your signature and your co-operation when it comes to getting the child away from the property without being seen. Your son will have a new identity and a new life without you in it. One that precludes any contact with you in future years.'

'Take him.' She spoke with no hesitation. 'Keep him safe if you can. Let him grow to become his own man—there's freedom in that, and choice. He could go to school, make friends with other children. I tried to get him to make friends, but he's too used to being with adults…he's never been anything but home-schooled.' She shook her head. 'The child thinks he's too sick for regular school. He's not. He was home-schooled because of his father's protectiveness and paranoia.'

'Under the circumstances, I guess the paranoia was warranted.'

'All I'm saying is that if he stops being Antonov's son, Celik can go to school. He can choose who he wants to be.' She looked sad suddenly. 'He won't get the chance to start over if he stays with me.'

'You *do* care about him?'

'No! Not enough to change my life. There's a difference between wanting someone to have a chance and caring about them.'

'Do you need more time to make a decision?'

She shook her head and turned away. 'No. Take him now. Take him away. I don't care.'

'Do you like yellow tulips?'

Her gaze met his in the mirror above the mantelpiece

as she poured herself a shot glass full of cognac and swallowed it. 'They're a little common.'

'Once a year, on this date, you'll receive a bunch of yellow tulips. A message, if you will, that your son is alive and well.'

Once upon a time Jared would never have thought to offer anyone that kind of solace. These days he better understood that some situations could be beyond a person's capacity to deal with them.

'You really don't have to do that.'

'I'll do it once. Should you refuse the delivery, you won't get any others.'

'Will you take the boy with you now?'

'Before six this evening—yes.'

'You have my thanks.' She shrugged, elegant, unapologetic, and whimsical again now that her life had been rearranged to her liking. She crossed to the window and drew the curtains aside. 'They watch my house all the time now. Two from below. One from a house across the canal. There may be more.'

'There *are* more. But I've got this. May I see the boy now?'

'Take the stairs to the top floor. He's in the room on the left. You can't miss it. His tutor is with him.' She shot him a wry smile. 'It's school time.'

Jared climbed the stairs, opened the first door to the left and watched the solemn-eyed little boy's face light up with relief.

'Jimmy!'

'Hey there, champ. How's it going?' was all he had time to say before his arms were full of boy.

'And you are...?' enquired the steel-haired matron sitting at a desk filled with books.

'Just passing through.' Jared smiled his most charming smile and watched the older woman's eyes start to thaw. He looked down at Celik next and shot the boy a grin. 'According to your mother you have five minutes of school left before we can break you out of here and go have some fun,' he said in Russian.

'Schooling is important,' the teacher said, clearly having no trouble at all understanding Jared's somewhat thick northern Russia accent. And then she offered them both a smile. 'But maybe today we will finish early, no? Maybe just this once.'

By the time darkness fell Jared and Celik were in the basement of the old canal house and Jared was busy removing the narrow window that sat just above the waterline from its hinges.

'Remember what I told you.' Jared crouched down and held the boy's gaze. 'We're going through the window and then we're going for a swim using scuba gear. It's just like the snorkelling gear you used to use, only better.'

'Like what you used when you checked the hull for bombs. You showed me.'

'Exactly like that. But it's going to be dark underwater and you won't be able to see much.'

'And I'm going to be clipped to you.'

'That's right. And we'll only be this far under the water.' Jared's spread his arms about a meter or so wide and then shortened it to half that before lengthening the distance again. 'So the moment you want to go to the surface you tug on my arm and up we go. Got that?'

The boy nodded.

'And what does this mean?' Jared continued the drill,

commanding the little boy's attention with his voice and eyes as he made the universal sign for okay with his fingers.

'It means I'm okay.'

'When we come up to the surface—and we will a few times—that's the signal I want to see. It'll tell me that you're ready to go back under again. Okay? Make the sign.'

He held up his own curled fingers as an example. Celik made the sign and Jared nodded.

'Good. Are you ready?'

The boy nodded enthusiastically, and Jared picked him up and stood him on the bench he'd placed below the window. They watched together as a long, many-seated, shallow-bottomed tourist boat stalled right in front of the little window. The pilot would slip over-board and then the boat would catch fire and provide them with some smoke and cover. Bless Damon and his remote management skills.

'Remember when I told you that a boat was going to help hide us while we slide out the window and into the water? That's the boat. And it's going to blow up now.'

Celik's eyes grew big and round.

Yeah, not a sentence a seven-year-old boy heard every day… Not even Antonov's son.

The explosion was a good one. The boat went up in flames, accompanied by a roil of black smoke. Jared took the window out and hoisted himself through it and into the inky black water, and then motioned for Celik to come. It helped that the boy could swim like a fish and looked upon this as an adventure. It also helped that one of Antonov's thugs had shown him as a six-year-old how scuba gear worked and had let the boy play around with it in a swimming pool before Antonov had put a stop to it.

The scuba gear he'd set in place earlier was still there. Less than thirty seconds later they were two feet underwater and swimming away from the blaze. Jared kept them close to the side of the canal and brought them to the surface beneath the shadows of the nearest bridge. He wanted to see that okay sign.

The kid was like an eel in the water, and when Jared gave him the sign the kid nodded vigorously, wrapped an arm around his neck and signalled right back.

So under they went again.

Two more times they surfaced, and soon enough came upon a row of houseboat hulls. Jared started counting them off. Six—and then a sharp right into an adjoining canal.

They were halfway through the turn when another boom sounded—a boom that shook the water. That didn't bode well. Forward progress suddenly became a whole lot more difficult, with water flowing swiftly in the opposite direction, and Jared clung with all his strength to the canal wall.

That secondary explosion was neither his nor Damon's doing.

Something to worry about.

Their last crawl along the side of the houseboat hulls took as much time as the rest of the swim put together, but eventually they surfaced again. Every muscle in Jared's arms and shoulders was screaming with the weight of Celik and the drag of the water.

This time they'd surfaced next to a ladder that was half hidden between a houseboat and the canal wall.

Jared wasted no time in getting the scuba gear off them and sending Celik up the ladder first.

'There's a towel waiting for you. Grab it and get warm.'

Moments later they were in the bowels of a comfortably shabby tourist houseboat and Jared was turning lights on.

'Are we good?'

Celik nodded, his eyes bright and his hair sticking up in tufts. 'Did we lose them? The bad men?'

'Yes. Jump in the shower and get warmed up while I put some soup on. Then I'm going to tell you a story about a little boy who never knew he had an aunt. An aunt who loved him very much, even though they'd never met. An aunt who wanted nothing more than to meet this little boy named Celik and help him to grow up healthy and happy and strong. Do you like the sound of that story?

Celik nodded.

'Good. Because next time I tell it I'm going to add speedboats, aeroplanes, sleepy mice and penguins.'

Rowan stood in front of the stern-faced grey-eyed man and stared down at a picture of what had once been an elegant Amsterdam canal house and was now little more than a pile of rubble, courtesy of some kind of explosion or bomb. The owner of the house—one Cerise Fallon—had not been injured in the explosion, but according to her there had been two others in the house at the time of the incident. A client, whose details had been lost along with her phone, and her seven-year-old son.

The next picture in the pile showed a picture of a beautiful woman standing in darkness, staring up at her burning house, her face lit by the nearby flames. Her tears looked convincing.

'Two days ago you asked me if you could brief Jared West on a situation involving Antonov's son,' said Rowan's boss. 'Know anything about this?'

'No, sir. I know nothing about this.'

'You expect me to believe that?'

'I never briefed Jared. I haven't been able to get hold of him. Have they found any bodies yet? Her son? The body of the client?'

'Not yet.'

'Then how do we know this isn't something that the Dutch authorities set up in order to spirit the child away? With the mother's full co-operation?'

'We don't.'

'Do we know what caused the explosion?'

'From what we can gather a boat caught fire outside the house. And then someone shot a grenade into a first-floor window. There's a Dutch forensics and recovery team working on it now.'

'A grenade?' Rowan winced.

'Was it West?' he asked again.

'I don't know.' Nothing but the truth.

'You said you hadn't been able to contact him. How many times did you try?'

'I called his number immediately after I spoke to you about the case two days ago. My assistant has been trying to get hold of him ever since.'

'And your inability to reach him didn't make you suspicious?'

'He's just bought a yacht. I thought—' Rowan stopped. There was no point continuing.

'You presumed?'

'Yes, sir, I presumed to know where he was.'

'Get him in here, Director. Preferably tonight. Make me believe that Jared West had nothing to do with this.'

'Yes, sir, I'll try.'

When Rowan still couldn't raise Jared she called his sister.

'Rowan!'

Lena sounded pleased to hear from her. Lazy Saturday afternoon drinks down by the river last weekend had a lot to answer for.

'You'd better make it Director Farringdon, Lena. This isn't a social call. I'm looking for Jared.'

'He took the boat out storm-chasing,' Lena offered, a whole lot more carefully. 'He does that.'

'Are you prepared to swear to that in court?'

Silence.

'If I send the coastguards out looking for him are they going to find him?'

More silence.

'Is there *any* chance at all that he can put in an appearance down here before tomorrow morning?'

'How about I get him to call you?' said Lena.

And Rowan felt her heart break, just a little bit, because any faint hope she'd had that Jared wasn't involved in this was rapidly dwindling.

'That's really not going to be good enough.'

'I'm sure he'll do his best.'

'Thanks.' Rowan hung up.

She was pretty sure he'd already done it.

Three days later there were still no bodies and Jared still hadn't called. On the fourth day the authorities advised that two bodies had been found. One as yet unidentified male and Celik Antonov.

For the first time in her career Rowan stopped all calls, sat back in her fancy leather chair and tried to remember how to breathe.

Sam stood in the doorway, her expression uncertain. 'Director, shall I send Jared West's identification details to the Dutch authorities?'

'No.' It was barely a croak. 'Let them do the work. We flag nothing. We have no knowledge of this. And, Sam? Cancel my appointments for the afternoon. I think I'm just going to go…home.'

She felt a sting in her eyes as Sam nodded and shut the door behind her. She *wouldn't* let tears fall here, in this place. It wasn't professional.

Think, Rowan. Think about this. Nothing was certain…even the child's supposed death.

Theory one: the Dutch authorities had spirited Celik Antonov away somewhere and were misleading them all. Oh, she liked that theory.

Theory two: young Celik had indeed lost his life, but the unidentified body was not Jared's. Rowan hated this theory, but it was better than the third.

Theory three: Jared was dead. Celik—dead. And a wrong call by her—back when Jared had wanted to go check on the boy—had contributed to their downfall.

If that was indeed Jared lying there in a body bag…

If it was.

So Jared had gone to see the boy—what then? What had gone wrong?'

Rowan wrapped her arms tightly around her middle and tried not to rock back and forth. She couldn't *be* this bereft. It wasn't possible. How could she have fallen so hard and so fast for Jared West when she'd only had the tiniest taste of him? A handful of stolen nights and a couple of meals—that was all. Intense when they were together, but it wasn't as if they'd been sharing each other's lives for a dozen years or more.

She hadn't been witness to his life for very long at all. She couldn't be in love with him. She just couldn't.

Trembling, she picked up the phone and dialled a number that she'd memorised days ago. 'Lena?'

'Rowan?' She sounded uncertain. 'I mean, Director...'

'Yes. They're saying that Celik Antonov is dead and that an unidentified male died with him. They're saying they have the bodies.' Rowan barely recognised the sound of her own voice. 'Tell me that you know where Jared is. Tell me you've spoken to him.'

'I've spoken to him,' Lena said instantly.

Rowan choked on a moan.

'Rowan? Director Farringdon? Do you hear me? I spoke to Jared not two hours ago. Whoever they have in that body bag, it's not my brother. I *know* this.'

Rowan couldn't speak. Her eyes were on fire and her throat kept trying to close. She couldn't breathe.

'Rowan, *talk* to me.'

'No one's—no one can find him.'

'He does that. I couldn't find him once for almost two years. I'm going to kill him. I told him to contact you. I *told* him.'

'No—it's—' She tried to pull herself together and couldn't.

'Director—?'

'I'll let you go.' A feeble end to a misguided phone call. 'I have another call coming in.'

Liar.

Desolation warred with relief as Rowan put the phone gently back in its cradle and then put her head in both hands and dug her fingers into her scalp until it hurt. Lena said she'd spoken to Jared, and Rowan believed her. He was alive.

He just hadn't seen fit to return her calls.

She made herself small and quiet—found that place deep down inside where she'd retreated so often as a child, that little dark hole where she could put herself back together again, piece by piece, until she was whole again.

Jared was alive. That was a block right there to build upon. Jared was alive and all she had to do now was sort out her private feelings for him and keep them separate from what was required of her professionally.

The Dutch were saying they had bodies. What good was it going to do anyone if she went sleuthing and discovered that this was a fabrication? What good would it do to confront Jared as to his whereabouts these past few days? Did she really want to know? Occasionally it was preferable simply to remain ignorant.

She'd know anyway. The minute she saw him again she'd know whether or not he'd had anything to do with Celik's demise or disappearance.

She'd send him that report about the two bodies, and if that didn't get him in here, spitting fire and glaring daggers…if that didn't get him roaring at her for not letting him go check on the boy two weeks earlier…

As for the rest of her relationship with him…

Deep down inside she started to curl in on herself again—so little spine, so weak and pathetic.

No need to be in love with a man she'd only known a few weeks.

No need to mourn the loss of a connection that had never been there in the first place.

He didn't trust her, and maybe she didn't trust him, and without at least some level of trust there was nothing worth having.

She'd needed him to call her this week and share something. His actions, his whereabouts. She'd have even gratefully accepted the briefest of calls just to let her know that he was still breathing.

But no.

He'd offered nothing.

Jared flew into Canberra dead tired but determined to see Rowan. Damon had forwarded him the press release from the Dutch, citing Celik and an unknown male dead, case closed and no more questions.

Celik's mother had probably told them of his involvement by now, but that was all they knew. Jared had told them nothing, so whatever game they were playing... he wasn't in on it. No one knew where Celik was now. As far as Jared was concerned no one ever needed to.

He took a taxi to the ASIS building and talked his way past the front desk. His presence *had* been requested by the director of Section Five after all.

Several days ago now.

Rowan's trusty assistant sat at the outer desk as usual, headphones on and fingers flying across the keyboard. It made his silent approach easier, and he was almost upon her before she looked up from her work. Her eyes widened at first, and then narrowed alarmingly. No welcome in them whatsoever as she slid her headphones off and stared at him in silence.

'Hey, Sam. Is she in?'

'If by *she* you mean Director Farringdon, then, no. Not in.'

Okay, maybe he should try that again. 'May I make an appointment to see the director, please?'

'Sweet manners, but you'll still have to wait your turn. How about—?' Sam turned her attention back to her computer screen. 'Friday week?'

'Seriously? She left a message saying she wanted to see me.'

'That was last week, when she was being hauled over the coals for a stunt some fool pulled in Amsterdam. Two dead, apparently.'

Jared scowled. 'I've seen the report.'

'Have you, now? And yet it still took you three days to put in an appearance? Where have you been, Mr West?'

'Busy.'

'Aren't we all? The director's not here and she no longer needs to see you. I'll let her know you've been in.' She slipped her headphones back on, dismissing him. 'You know the way out. You've walked it enough.'

Yes, he should have called her. He'd been somewhere in Poland when Damon had relayed her first message. He'd thought about calling her and lying outright, but that hadn't sat well with him. He'd thought about calling her and coming clean, but he honestly hadn't known what she would do with the information.

She was a director for the Australian Secret Intelligence Service. She'd have been obliged to hand that information over to them. She couldn't tell them what she didn't know.

Surely she would know that he'd been protecting her?

Surely she could see that a new start had been imperative for Celik and that someone had to organise it and that the best man for the job had been him?

Surely…

And even if they did have differences of opinion when it came to the way he'd handled the situation, surely she'd hear him out?

Wouldn't she?

He had every confidence in her ability to bring a thoughtful, rational approach with her to their current predicament. That was why he was currently pacing the pavement outside her apartment block like a downtrodden preacher without an audience.

He saw her drive past and into the car park beneath the building. He knew he was in trouble when she walked back out of the driveway and started towards him. She looked older tonight, in the shadows of the evening. As if her own light had dimmed in the week since he'd last seen her.

It had only been a week.

Okay, a week and a half—and he'd got here as soon as he could.

She stopped in front of him and simply stood there and looked at him—and the tilt of her lips might have been a smile but for the complete lack of a smile behind them.

He tucked his hands in his pockets and tried not to worry.

'You're looking good,' she said. 'You always do.'

Okay, he had no idea where she was going with this. Nowhere good. 'I got here as soon as I could.'

'You heard about Celik Antonov's death?'

'I heard about his supposed death. Not sure I believe it,' he offered carefully, and watched as what little light she had left went out altogether.

'I tried to call you,' she said quietly. 'I was hoping to bring you in on the case before the situation worsened. I thought you'd want in on it. Did you not get my messages?'

'They caught up with me a couple of days back.' He opted for the half-truth, knowing as the words spilled from his lips that his explanation wouldn't satisfy her.

'And the reason they didn't catch up with you before then…?'

'I switched phones and left the old phone at home.'

At least that was the truth. He hadn't known that Rowan had been trying to contact him practically from the moment he'd left for Europe.

'I should have called you sooner, though. I just wasn't altogether sure who I'd get. The woman I have a relationship with or the ASIS director.'

'Something we might have discussed had you rung,' she said bleakly. 'Why couldn't you have given me that opportunity? Do you trust me that little?'

'I was trying to *protect* you.'

'In that case, keep up the good work. Go home, Jared. And if you don't have one of those go wherever it is that you go when you don't want to be found.'

'Rowan, please. Hear me out.'

'No. I don't want to hear what you have to say. Not in relation to any case that has just been closed. Not in relation to anything else.'

'We have a *relationship*,' he insisted.

'No. A relationship requires some small measure of trust and respect for the other person's feelings. We had sex.'

'We had more than that.'

'I thought you were dead.'

Okay, so there *was* that…

'I go into work and have a report come in on Celik Antonov's situation. I immediately ask for permission to bring you in on it. I call and you don't answer. Two days later I get hauled over the coals for a situation that I know nothing about and I try to call you again. Still no answer. And then it gets worse. I get a report over my desk that Celik and an unidentified man are dead. I sit there and I wonder, and I try not to fall apart. Finally I call your sister and tell her that I haven't heard from you, that I have this report on my desk. And she *knows* what I'm thinking without me having to say a word and she throws me a bone… She tells me that you're not dead— and at least that's something, right? You're *alive*.' Her voice cracked. 'That was two days ago.'

'Ro—

'No! Do you have *any* idea how I felt? One phone call, Jared. You could have told me you were in Antarctica and I wouldn't have pushed you for anything else. But you never made the call. You didn't trust me with *any* information at all. How do you think that made me feel?'

'Rowan, let's take this inside.' He was shaking. 'Let me explain.'

But she went toe to toe with him instead. 'What's to explain? You don't trust me. You left me and I didn't even know where you'd gone. Where—in any of this—is

your consideration for my feelings for *you*? Anywhere?
Because I can't see it.'

'I can do better. I *will*. There won't *be* another situation like the one we were just in. We can do this,
Rowan—please. I'm sorry.'

'I'm sorry too. Because I so badly wanted to believe
in us. But you don't get to diminish me like that—make
me feel as if I barely exist.'

The tears that spilled down her cheeks gutted him.

'I won't let you.'

'Rowan, don't—

'*No!* Go away, Jared. I don't want to hear it. I'm sorry,
but we're done.'

CHAPTER FOURTEEN

RIGHTEOUS ANGER MIGHT have helped Rowan hang together long enough to do what had had to be done, but
it didn't make for good company. She spent one night
locked in misery and the next day and night functioning
on autopilot, wishing Jared West would disappear from
her memory—only it wasn't happening.

He'd put in another appearance at Section and she'd
immediately kicked him over to Corbin, who'd questioned him about the Amsterdam incident.

Not surprisingly, Jared had denied all involvement.

She'd watched the interview from behind a one-way
mirror, along with the steely-eyed man who oversaw
all the sections, and at the end of the interview he'd
turned to her and asked if she believed the story West
was spinning.

'Do you?' she'd asked quietly, but hadn't waited for
his answer.

She cut her work-day short and went to see her grandfather.

He was in his garden, as usual, pampering runner
beans, dahlias, and his fifty-year-old tortoise, Veronica.
He smiled when he saw her.

'Granddaughter.' The smile dimmed somewhat when

he got a good look at her. 'What gives? Because you are three hours and one day early for our dinner date.'

'It's been a hard week. I wanted to touch base with my favourite tortoise.'

She spared a glance for her grandfather's pond. Yep, there she was. Half out of the pond, neck at full stretch, and beady eyes trained on the latest goings-on. Nothing escaped Veronica.

'Problem at work?'

'There was. But it's been resolved.'

'To your satisfaction?'

'To the satisfaction of some.'

'But not you?'

'Can't have everything.' She'd learned that as a child. 'Do you think I have abandonment issues?'

Her grandfather's eyes narrowed. 'That's quite a question…'

'Are you likely to need tea, coffee or any other fortifying beverage before giving me an answer?'

'Tea and cake might help it along some.'

He gathered up his walking stick and headed inside and Rowan followed. Not until they were both settled at the little kitchen table by the window did he return to the question.

'Who let you down?'

'A man. A young, impulsive one.'

'A good man?'

'Yes.' It was true, even though the word burned on her tongue. 'In many ways…yes. He's a little reckless.'

'You're a little cautious.'

'I'm not cautious at all. I just like to plan ahead and cover my bases.'

He smiled slightly. 'And everyone else's.'

Okay, maybe he had a point. 'Remember how I mentioned that we were bringing someone in from deep undercover? His name's Jared West and he's the one I'm having trouble with.'

'In a personal sense or a professional one?'

Rowan sipped at her coffee. 'Both. Although he no longer works for ASIS. He finished up a couple of weeks ago—as soon as his debrief was done.'

'How long was he undercover for?'

'Two years. He was in the employ of an international arms dealer.'

'Antonov?' Her grandfather huffed a dry laugh. 'He brought down the Antonov operation?'

'Yes. And left Antonov's son exposed. The boy was placed with his mother, but she couldn't cope with the legacy Antonov left behind. I think Jared relocated the child. Put him somewhere safe. That's what I'd like to think. But I don't know.'

Rowan shrugged and traced doodles on the tablecloth with her fingertip.

'I got too close to him, Grandfather. I let myself care for the man and then he went no contact. He just…disappeared without a word and I didn't know where he was.' Her heart thumped hard. 'I *hate* that.'

'I know you do. Did Jared West have a reason for going no contact?'

'You mean besides not wanting anyone to know what he was up to?'

'Plausible deniability, Rowan. You know how it's done. This way you know nothing. And you continue to know nothing.'

'And then there's what would be best for the child. I

know it was playing on his mind. The child needed witness protection. A new life. We could have arranged it.'

'Although possibly not to Jared West's satisfaction,'
her grandfather said dryly.

'Possibly not.'

Her grandfather regarded her solemnly. 'Did he know
that you might react badly to not knowing where he
was? Did you tell him about your upbringing in those
early years?'

'I— No. I don't really talk about that.'

'Maybe you should.'

Rowan picked up her coffee mug and took a deep
gulp. 'So I'm asking again,' she continued doggedly. 'In
this case, given what I've told you, do you think I have
abandonment issues?'

'Yes. You developed them as a child and for a time
you let them rule you. But you're not a child now.'

'I sent him away.'

'So get him back.'

'I suggested he stay away.'

'Can a person not admit that they were wrong?'

'*Was* I wrong?'

'Rowan. I'm not all-knowing and all-seeing, no matter how wise I like to think I am. Only you can answer
that one.'

Jared hadn't given up. He never gave up when he wanted
something badly enough. He figured it would come as
no surprise to the director that he would give her a couple of days to cool off and then he'd be back. With food
that might tempt her to stop and take a bite. With another apology—a bigger one—and an explanation if she

wanted it. With promises if she wanted those, and every intention of keeping them.

He kept his word.

She saw him the minute she walked away from the ASIS building at nine p.m. Hard not to, given that he was standing there leaning against his car. She'd agreed to give him five minutes of her time. Or Sam had agreed on Rowan's behalf. Either way, she headed towards him without hesitation.

'I probably have half an hour left in me before my brain gives up in exhaustion,' she said quietly. 'Would you like to join me at the Marble Bar?'

It was a white-collar work haunt, connected to an international hotel chain, and it was just around the corner. The booths were private and the lights were low. They could have a relatively private conversation there—of a sort.

'Sure.'

He opened the car door for her, wanting nothing more than to gather her up, wrap his arms around her and bury his head in the curve of her neck and stay there until she softened. Her body would remember him. He could coax capitulation from her, he was sure.

Instead he kept his manners in place and tried to ignore the silent simmer between them as they made their way to the bar and found a booth and placed their drinks order. Decaf coffee for them both. He added a couple of side dishes for good measure. Lamb pieces in a yoghurt sauce. Rice balls.

'I made a promise,' he began. 'To a seven-year-old. When the world around us was burning I promised that I would look out for him and I have. I will continue to look out for him from afar. I'd rather you didn't ask, but if you do I *will* tell you everything.'

'I'm not asking.' She held his gaze. 'The case is closed.'

'Which kind of just leaves the promises I want to make to you going forward.'

He watched as tears gathered in her eyes and threatened to fall. She looked utterly miserable, and so far away from him in that moment that she broke his heart.

'Don't cry. Don't. I can't stand it.'

'Talk,' she said raggedly. 'I'm listening now. I wasn't the last time I saw you.'

Where to start?

'I should have told you I was heading off and wouldn't be in contact for a while. I thought the less you knew of my movements last week the better, but clearly that isn't going to work for us.'

'I used to wake up all the time when I was small. New country, big house with staff, and my parents would be gone. No one ever told me anything. I used to feel so invisible. I still react badly to feeling invisible.'

'I have *never* thought of you as invisible. I walk into a room and you're the one I look for. As for those bodies that the Dutch claim exist… That was *never* part of my plan. I knew you'd be wondering what had gone on with the boy and I thought to protect you by telling you nothing. I knew you were looking for me and I still didn't call. I would have called had I known what I know now. If ever there's a next time, I will call. There can be ground rules. Never leave without saying goodbye. Never stay away without getting in touch. Never let you think that I don't love you. Because I love you so much.'

He'd always thought that those simple little words of love would be hard for him to say.

They weren't.

'I love you.'

'You do?' She curled her hand around her coffee cup and wouldn't look at him. 'You could have anyone.'

'Good—because I choose you.'

'Someone beautiful.'

'You *are* beautiful. And don't say I could have someone young, who'd want to give me a family. I know what I want. From the moment I saw you that was me gone. Please, Rowan. Give me another chance.'

'Okay.'

He could barely hear her.

'You kind of had me at *I made a promise to a seven-year-old*. And you kept it.'

Finally she looked up at him and he allowed himself to hope.

'Would you like to take this somewhere more private? My place?'

'Or my place here? You haven't seen that one yet. Or the apartment? Wherever you feel the most comfortable.'

'My place. Or— No. There's no food in the fridge.'

'Do we care? Are we caring about that?'

'Not even ice cream. I ate it in one sitting. When I thought you were dead.'

'Perfectly reasonable.' He had sisters. He could handle this.

'I cursed you to straight to hell.'

'Harsh, but fair.'

'You do realise the power balance will tumble back and forward between us all the time?'

He smiled at that. 'I'm looking forward to it.'

'And my work—we're going to need some ground rules when it comes to what I can discuss.'

'I can understand that. I'm good with that. I have a couple of ongoing projects that I won't discuss either. We can *do* this. We just need to keep the communication lines open when it comes to what we can't discuss. I can tell you I'm off to visit the penguins in Antarctica every now and then. Call you from an iceberg.'

He spun some money on the table, more than enough to cover the drinks they'd ordered, and stood.

'I really need to hold you now. And we need to take it somewhere private, because my self-control is all but shot.'

She came around to his side and pressed up against him.

He'd never known a woman's touch that could both soothe and inflame him until this touch. He never wanted any other woman at his side but this one.

'My place is closest,' she whispered. 'We could go there, and I could gather the courage to stand naked before you and tell you that I love you right back.'

'Good plan.'

They made it outside and to the car door before he gave in to temptation and kissed her.

'You have no idea how much I admire your forward-thinking right now.'

'And then you can get naked too—I can help you with that—and then you tell me you love me again.' She smiled dulcetly. 'And make me believe it.'

CHAPTER FIFTEEN

THE LITTLE YACHT rode the waves with panache, even if the interior cushions *were* still the colour of mustard. Rowan had the wheel, and Jared trimmed the sails, and together they made the craft skim through the Pacific like a hot knife through butter.

Put Rowan and Jared together and they could usually conquer anything. This they had discovered in the six months they'd been together.

It had been the happiest, most adventurous and fulfilling six months of her life.

Jared's siblings had accepted her without question, even if she was ten years older than Jared and destined to remain childless. Jared's choice—Jared's business. They trusted him, as she trusted him, to do right by all of them.

He was that kind of man.

He'd taken on two more retrieval jobs since Celik, with Rowan's full knowledge and unofficial support. Rowan had been his muse and Damon had been his handler during the runs. Jared had called her every day and talked about penguins and icecaps. He'd returned bearing fresh scars and seeking her touch, and she was no longer worried that she wasn't the one for him.

Not when every glance and every touch confirmed it.

Three times now Rowan had asked Management if she could call him in on a case. They'd let her bring him up to date and together they'd brainstormed. On one turbulent occasion he'd even gone into the field and fixed it.

Yes, she'd been worried. Yes, she'd handed over case management to Corbin on that one. But she'd been Corbin's shadow and there'd been security and reassurance in knowing that she had every detail of his whereabouts and actions at her fingertips.

Action and thought. They could slice and dice these two elements every which way and still manage to make things work.

'Hey, Jared? Where are we going?' she called as he tightened the mainsail and she adjusted their course.

'East.' He could still be insanely fuzzy when it came to details. 'We'll just tack our way out.'

'Yes, but *why*?' If they kept going east they'd end up in Chile.

'The wind, Ro, the *wind*! Think of the ride back in on the turnaround.'

And then there was the fun in him. The daredevil with the mile-wide grin and eyes the colour of the ocean.

She had a proposal for him.

'Hey, Jared? I had a talk with Management yesterday and they offered me a new position. Complete autonomy. Black operations. Specialist team.'

'Really?' Suddenly the sail snapped tight and he tied it off and made his way back to her. 'What was your answer?'

'I declined the offer and gave them a counter-offer to consider.'

His arms came around her from behind, crossing over her waist, making her feel treasured.

'This is why I love you,' he murmured. 'What did you tell them?'

'That I wanted to finish up in my position and go free-lance. Or a part-time position. And that I would bring my own carefully selected team to the table with me when required.'

Jared leaned forward so that he could see her face. 'You *what*?'

'I know. Most beautiful counter-offer ever. They accepted it.'

'But—your career… The one you've dreamed about since you were a teenager. The one you've worked all your life towards.'

'I had a look at where else there was left for me to go and I didn't much care for the view. The career I have now has got me to the point where I can name my own terms. There's nothing more I want from it. I'm on two months' notice.'

'Are you sure?'

'Very sure.'

'And this team of yours? Who does that involve?'

'I mentioned no names and they didn't ask. I made no promises whatsoever on your behalf. Still…if you're interested…I'm thinking three, maybe four jobs per year. Specialist retrieval jobs that need our combined touch. It'd let us be selective. It'd give me more time for you. And this.'

'I'm in.' His arms tightened around her. 'Ro, are you sure?'

'I'm sure. I don't want to see you on Wednesday

nights and weekends any more. I'm greedier than that. I want more.'

'Where do you want to live?'

'On the beach,' she said instantly, for she'd fallen in love with it. 'Somewhere near here—close to Lena and Trig and to Damon's beach house. This is the place for us.'

'What about your grandfather?'

'He loves it here. I think he could be persuaded to visit regularly.'

'And your parents?'

'I figure we'd see them less often.' She tried to accommodate them—she did try. But there was still a lot of distance to bridge. 'I have some money saved. I can sell my apartment. I can put in my fair share and then we can do a budget and go looking.'

'Always with the details...' But he was smiling when he said it. 'I'm in. I am *so* in.'

'There's one more thing.'

'I'm listening.'

She took a deep breath and put it out there. Not a little thing. A really big thing that would need serious consideration and discussion.

'Want to make a baby with me?'

Time stopped. Wind rattled the sails and the little boat shuddered. There could be no turning back from this.

He wanted to. She could see it in his face and she had never felt so much happiness. No matter what happened when it came to babies, and the likelihood of them, she would always have this moment and this decision.

'Yes,' he growled, and bent.

The next thing she knew she'd been upended over

Jared's shoulder and was staring at his faded-jeans-clad, wholly delectable ass.

'Now. Right now.' Jared West—man of action. 'Let's do this.'

And she was laughing even as she caught hold of the stair railings and resisted his downward motion. 'But, Jared, don't you want to think about this for more than two seconds?'

'Don't need to.'

'I'm older. It might not work.'

'Then we'll die trying.'

'And then there's the genius genes. If our child turns out to be super-smart, that's *your* responsibility.'

'No problem. I'll farm him out to Damon.'

'Him? *Him?*'

'Or her. *Them.*'

Her man was nothing if not adaptable, and they were *doing* this. Jared *wanted* this. She had her answer.

'So we're doing this now?'

'Yes!'

Oh, hell yes.

But it simply wasn't in her nature to make it easy on him. 'But, Jared, what about this pretty boat? The wheel, the sails, the *wind*?'

'It's good,' he said. 'It's all good. Trust me.'

And she did.

EPILOGUE

THE WALLS WERE round and the furnishings were soft. A posy of lavender sat in a cheerful yellow vase in the corner. There were two beds in the room and Jared had already pushed them together to make a big one. It was the latest and greatest in the private hospital's maternity wing—overnight rooms for new families. Theirs even had a sliding door leading out to a tiny private court-yard surrounded by screening hedges and featuring a bird bath complete with inquisitive sparrows.

Up until recently soothing whale music had echoed through the room, but the music had been stopped at Rowan's request. Any more whales and she was going to reach for the nearest harpoon, she'd said

His daughter—the one snugged in tightly to Rowan's chest—didn't know about whales, lavender or hospital rooms yet, and maybe she wouldn't remember this room full of aunties and uncles and one sleeping cousin, but they were all here. Every one of Jared's siblings and their partners was here to celebrate the latest, littlest addition to their family group and Jared was grateful.

Yesterday's labour had been hard and long. Rowan had been exhausted and Jared had been more so, thor-oughly traumatised by all the things about birth that he couldn't control and a midwife who'd reassured him that everything was going exactly as it should. All that pain and the pushing—exactly as it should have been. Heaven help them all.

And then Rowan had delivered a sticky and squalling baby girl and Jared had taken one look at her and fallen in love all over again. Seven pounds and eight ounces of little baby girl. His to love, treasure and honour. No setbacks for either baby or mother.

The midwife had placed the baby skin to skin atop her mother's heart and Rowan had looked up, her eyes shining, and said, 'C'mere...'

And now he was done. So enamoured of his girls that he had barely been able to see daylight when it had arrived this morning. And if his family teased him about the expression of wonder currently stuck on his face, then so be it. They didn't *know*.

Okay, Damon knew. Damon and Ruby had a son on the ground—a laughing little guy who had taken his first wobbly steps not two days ago. Maybe they knew this feeling better than he did. Still...

Those two...right there on the bed...the beautiful woman with the funny face and the ears that maybe stuck out just a little, and the baby girl with her eyes currently fixed on her daddy's shirt...they were his world.

Poppy and Seb were going to wait a while when it came to children. Damon and Ruby were planning another one. Lena and Trig—Lena for whom children were no longer an option—currently had the care and feeding of a twelve-year-old boy.

Jared had looked to Lena with faint apology in his eyes when she'd first come into the room, with Trig not far behind, but she'd taken one look at him and launched herself at him, hugging him as much in warning as in love.

'Don't,' she'd said. 'Don't you dare spoil this moment with whatever guilt trip is in your head. You let me celebrate your little girl. Because I am going to celebrate this one, Jare. For *all* of us. I'm going to celebrate hard.'

Yeah… As far as family was concerned, his little girl had landed in a special one.

'So, this is…' He looked to Rowan and grinned foolishly. 'Mine.'

'What are you going to call her?' asked Lena.

'Damona,' said Damon instantly as he cradled his sleeping Thomas in his arms. 'Got a nice ring to it.'

'Stay away from Shakespeare,' Poppy—full name Ophelia—told him earnestly. 'And hallucinogenic flower names—stay away from those too.'

'I always liked your name,' Lena said to Poppy. 'It's pretty.'

'They might want a shrub name, in keeping with Rowan's,' offered Poppy's partner, Seb. 'Willow? Or Bay?'

'Pomona?' Poppy said. 'Meaning apple. She's also the Roman goddess of fruit.'

'Stay away from the fruit,' Jared's best friend, Trig, told him, and struggled to keep a straight face. 'In fact stay away from all the food groups. Honey, Ginger, Margarita…'

'Don't you listen to them, sweetheart,' said Rowan, covering the little girl's ears. 'They're all mad. I'll explain how *that* happened when you get older.'

Jared smirked and pushed the dozens of pillows surrounding Rowan aside so that he could slip in beside her on the bed. 'Tell me when they get too much and I'll move them on,' he murmured.

'I heard that,' said Lena. 'And you can try, but I'm not leaving until this baby has a name. Look at her—she's so perfect. She reminds me of—' Lena stopped and her eyes sought Jared's. 'A perfect little girl,' she finished softly. 'Rowan, what *are* you going to call her?'

'Jared and I had a deal. If the baby was a boy I got to choose the name. If we had a girl it was Jared's choice.' Laughing, dancing eyes turned towards him. 'You should put your family out of their misery.'

'I'm enjoying their misery,' he said, but he touched the pad of his thumb to his daughter's tiny head and then awkwardly cleared his throat. 'So…I…uh—it's a family name. Everybody: meet Claire…Claire Elizabeth Farringdon West. After our mother.'

Nothing but silence followed.

'Is everyone okay with that?' he asked gruffly.

Lena nodded and promptly burst into tears. Poppy soon followed.

'It's good,' said Damon, who'd never known their mother.

Damon's wife, Ruby, stepped close and silently put her arms around him and Thomas and both. 'Feels right.'

And then the midwife came in and took one look at all the teary-eyed visitors. Her steely gaze fell next on mother and baby. 'What's all this?'

'We just named her,' Rowan said. 'Meet Claire Elizabeth.'

'A fine name it is,' said the midwife. 'And all the crying is because…?'

'Because it's perfect,' said Lena as more tears threatened to fall.

'That's it for visiting hour,' said the midwife in a no-nonsense voice and opened the door wide, looking more than capable of pushing people through it should anyone dissent. 'This lovely family have had a hard night—all three of them. They need their rest.'

But Lena moved forward before she went out, her eyes faintly pleading as she caught Rowan's gaze. 'May I touch her?'

'Would you like to hold her?' offered Rowan.

So far only Jared had held her, apart from Rowan.

'No! I—I… Not yet. I just—' Lena stroked the tiny head and then pressed a kiss to the baby's crown. 'Okay, I'm done.'

'Hey, Claire?' Jared rumbled softly. 'That was your aunt. She's probably going to teach you how to skydive.'

'And terrify your father,' Lena said. 'Consider it my gift to you.'

The midwife cleared her throat and Lena straightened.

'Congratulations. She's so beautiful—and so lucky to have you as parents. I know you'll be good.'

They all filtered out and the door closed behind them, leaving Jared and Rowan alone with their newborn.

'Have I told you how much I love you yet today?' he murmured as he settled back in beside Rowan.

'Yes.'

Good job.

'And I love *you*.'

'That's good to hear.'

He would never tire of hearing those words, or of needing this woman's love. He reached out and touched Claire's tiny hand, captivated all over again as his little girl wrapped tiny fingers around his big one and held on tight.

'Do you think she'd like to hear a story?'

'What about?'

'I have an extensive repertoire. Explosions, escapes, hair-raising adventures, espionage…'

'You should probably start small.'

Rowan looked ever so slightly incredulous, and he loved it that he could still put that look there. Never dull, this life of theirs. And right here, right now, it had never been more perfect.

'You want me to tell her about Veronica the tortoise and the garden hose?'

'It's a little raunchy for a newborn.' Rowan's smile said it all. 'Tell her the one about the sun in the sky, the slippery slide and the dancing penguins first.'

* * * * *

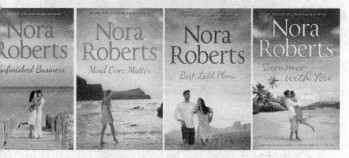

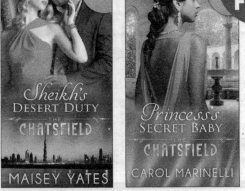

MILLS & BOON®

MODERN™

POWER, PASSION AND IRRESISTIBLE TEMPTATION

A sneak peek at next month's titles...

In stores from 17th April 2015:

- **The Sheikh's Secret Babies** – Lynne Graham
- **At Her Boss's Pleasure** – Cathy Williams
- **The Marakaios Marriage** – Kate Hewitt
- **The Greek's Pregnant Bride** – Michelle Smart

In stores from 1st May 2015:

- **The Sins of Sebastian Rey-Defoe** – Kim Lawrence
- **Captive of Kadar** – Trish Morey
- **Craving Her Enemy's Touch** – Rachael Thomas
- **The Hotel Magnate's Demand** – Jennifer Rae

Available at WHSmith, Tesco, Asda, Eason, Amazon and Apple

Just can't wait?
Buy our books online a month before they hit the shops!
visit www.millsandboon.co.uk

These books are also available in eBook format!

0208 6694 962

Join our *EXCLUSIVE* eBook club

0203 551 8171

Ola!
usrijus
U yusuf

FROM JUST £1.99 A MONTH!

Never miss a book again with our hassle-free eBook subscription.

★ Pick how many titles you want from each series with our flexible subscription

★ Your titles are delivered to your device on the first of every month

★ Zero risk, zero obligation!

There really is nothing standing in the way of you and your favourite books!

Start your eBook subscription today at www.millsandboon.co.uk/subscribe